If Memory Serves:

Stories from the Table

Food writing is frequently a repository for sentimentality and, as such, often forfeits honesty for tidy stories. The result is that we are robbed of the deep insight that the medium can achieve at its best. *If Memory Serves* refuses to fall into the trap of maudlin universality. Its global roster of writers expands boundaries and offers complicated, horrific and joyful stories about how they see themselves, their communities and the world.

— Thérèse Nelson, chef and founder of Black Culinary History

There is so much grief and sadness in this collection, with stories raw, beautiful and brilliantly written. The gravity of them pulled me in, and I was left yearning for my own deep connections and memories to the foods and people I love.

— Chris Smith, James Beard Award-winning author of *The Whole Okra*

I knew that I will be rereading these stories for years as soon as I turned the last page. Food memories are among our most potent and evocative, riling up our senses and recasting our experiences. Each of us understands what it is to remember. Each of us has feasted, hungered and craved. But only adroit writers can articulate those sensations, somehow translating thoughts and feelings into artful language that lasts. That is the gift to us from each writer in this collection.

— Sheri Castle, host of PBS' Emmy-winning show "The Key Ingredient"

Dominant narratives about food tend to revolve around tropes of connection and unity. There is celebration and love in this evocative anthology of short-form prose and poetry. But editor Cynthia Greenlee and these writers don't cower from our hardest and most complicated experiences: food that fends off crisis; food that leaves us yearning; and food that gives and refuses reconciliation. Then, there's the food that we didn't have and how the lack of it follows us through life and changes us at the core. *If Memory Serves* is a gorgeous, engaging read about how food intersects with the realest parts of our humanity and never really shakes us loose.

— Kim Foster, James Beard Award-winning author of *The Meth Lunches: Food and Longing in an American City*

IF MEMORY SERVES

Stories from the Table

GUEST EDITOR
Cynthia Greenlee

GOOD PRINTED THINGS

Editor:
Cynthia Greenlee

Copy Editor:
Mallory Corum

Cover Art:
KC Christmas

Cover Design:
Eli Cate

Interior Layout:
Eli Cate
Lib Ramos

First Edition
Printed in the United States of America
goodprintedthings.com
Greenville, South Carolina

ISBN: 979-8-9921993-6-9
LCCN: 2025950883

This project is funded in part by the Metropolitan Arts Council which receives support from the City of Greenville, BMW Manufacturing Company, and SEW Eurodrive.

Table of Contents

Memory resides in the sensory. We remember with our bodies, and our brains, tongues and noses perhaps more so than other organs. That's why we can recall, with the most exquisite and minute detail, the last supper with a loved one. And why, say, I remember that my farmer-grandfather, Bruce Daniels, who died when I was five, smelled of cured tobacco and South Carolina sunshine. Or why I smell chocolate when I think of his wife, my grandmother, Sylvester. She made these Titanic-sized cakes, with each layer of moist yellow cake resting on a sumptuous lake of hand-whipped frosting. And she warned her granddaughters to only entertain male suitors whose family would feed you two pieces of meat — and only two, ample good cuts would do — when courtship became serious enough that the families convened to talk intention. She was of marriageable age during the Depression, when hunger hollowed eyes and stomachs across the United States. She remembered that well into her 90s, even when her refrigerator was full.

It's hard to summarize what lies within these pages. I've been flailing for the right words to convey literary plenty and diversity. Smorgasbord? Tapas? Buffet? A box of chocolates to be grazed and sampled, according to your bookish taste? They all seemed so insultingly pedestrian, and contemporary food writing brims with enough vacuous, precious metaphor, as it is.

So I settle for simple description. There are essays, and the poets have shown up and shown out; publisher Lib Ramos and I naively didn't expect so much poetry or to be so taken in by it (I admit to a prose writer's bias). Selections talk about food through objects, food as labor, as women's work, as relationship glue, and that which tears us asunder. I can also tell you the contributors come from places far and places familiar: Palestine, Nigeria, Sweden, Tunisia, the U.S. South, Black America, immigrant communities, tribal nations, and, most of all, their own families.

We all come from somewhere, and identity animates much of the verse and prose in this collection. We can talk of identity here in these pages amid this age of book banning and escalating un-freedom; thank goodness for the small-but-mighty independent presses that have fed so much that is good in the world and the world of print. Many of the artists herein write about the people who have made them — human ingredients, as I say. There are stories of poignant and dysfunctional mothering; tender fathers and sexist patriarchs; intergenerational and cross-cultural learning; and how love and life blossom and how they can wither and die.

Grief is abundant here, and I think that's a lingering product of pandemic isolation and confusing, hateful times. Joy makes periodic and sometimes luminous appearances. Many of our writers have had to fashion lives from other "ingredients" when loved ones defaulted on the social contracts that shared DNA seems to imply. Food has often played a role in those painful recalibrations: meals not spent with family, Friendsgivings, trying to reconstruct beloved recipes and gatherings when people and memory fail. Memory itself is a fickle thing, influenced as much by desire and feeling as by fact.

Food writing need not be studded by the tired, triumphalist narratives that because we all eat, food is a great unifier. Here, you will read writing about hunger, both the physiological and mental effects of food scarcity. These wordsmiths also speak about hungers for acceptance, specific foods, some undefined something better. So what I'm trying to say is that many of these pieces are really about longing — for a place, an ancestor, innocence lost, a treat, or for a feeling. Reading these poems and essays, chosen from a bumper crop of almost 400 submissions, convinced me that longing is an under-rated emotion. We should speak — and write — about longing more.

— Dr. Cynthia Greenlee

PINK WORLD

She'd whip flavored gel into a frenzy in the blender and pour the results into heavy glass green goblets, until the middle shelf of the refrigerator was filled with paste swirls like so many little beehive hairdos. She kept her diet limited to three foods and switched them every three years. Potato skins were one. Pico de gallo was another. Tiny Pacific shrimp.

In one sense, it was not surprising since trauma is the secret source of selective eating. Those who can't control abuse coming out of a mouth can at least control what they put into their own mouths. Very toxic people, my grandparents. I know! Yet she remained sharp as a tack. Maybe everyone should consider a three-food diet as they age. My mother is in excellent, skinny shape.

Friendships in childhood began with a tour of the home. We are docents, showing off the rooms and collections, sometimes apologetic, sometimes proud. On the tour, I'd finish by opening our refrigerator to a pastel sea where normally milk and orange juice would sit. My friends, falling into the three basic categories of friends — the sophisticate, the empiricist, and the jerk — always wanted a sample. I should have suspected that would happen, but somehow it caught me by surprise. Prepubescence is like that stupid definition of stupidity — doing the same thing over and over and expecting different results. Together, we gazed in awe at the froth-topped globes. "Air has no calories," I always pointed out. She was terrified of calories, and I assumed everyone else was as well.

They all wanted a taste of pink world. I handed out spoons, and they dipped in, breaking the crust with a sound that was probably familiar to an ice fisherman. I stood by and watched as they would crunch in silence. The final pronouncement? *It's weird.* That's a word that means to be able to control fate. That's why it's used so frequently in grade school where one feels buffeted about by fate. Yet now — and this also never seemed to occur to me beforehand — there was one pink goblet less. She wasn't going to be happy about that. The dish wasn't complicated to make but neither was it fast to finish. Gelatin sets slower than permanents. I'd move items around, bottles, cans, bags of lettuce, tiny shrimp, to make up for the missing goblet. A life lesson I wish I'd absorbed better is that a globe of nothing can never be replaced.

I grew up a bit odd about food. I believe everyone is in their secret hearts. Nothing about our ingestion, our nourishment is truly universal. Our tongue is as individual as a thumb. The stacked glasses sometimes return to me, in spring, the airy season. The sound of a blender brings me so much comfort I'll stand inside the smoothie shop, pretending to be of several minds about what to order. If we are what we eat, I'm doomed. But if we are what we taste, I'm elevated. I know that a world floats above this world. You just open the door and there it is, beckoning in clouds of desire, truly in the pink.

IN GAZA, WE WERE NOT ALWAYS STARVING

Before the genocide, we used to eat at least three meals a day. Food was never something we questioned. It was part of our rhythm.

Every time I felt hungry, I scrolled through my phone's gallery — thick with photos of me and my best friend, Aya. We'd send each other photos that made us laugh and crave something sweet. We spent so much time looking through those memories, pausing at the little moments, the laughter, the food we loved before the genocide: shawarma meals, Syrian and Farshouha wraps, shawarma fatteh. Chicken cordon bleu, Alfredo, fajitas, crispy strips. Burgers, fries, kibbeh. We always saved room for dessert: cheesecake, tiramisu, Nutella pizza.

Now? I drink water — again and again — just to fool my stomach into feeling full. That's what "eating" means now. No taste. No choice. Just survival.

In Gaza, we were not always starving. We lived with fullness and choice. We cooked with care and celebrated flavors. I was picky but loved dishes that felt like home. Our tables were rich with dishes like maqluba, layered with fragrant rice and tender vegetables; musakhan, spiced with sumac and caramelized onions; makaronah, tossed in a rich tomato sauce; and maftoul, prepared for family gatherings. During Ramadan, the air was filled with the scent of soups, fresh salads, crispy sambousek, and golden falafel. Dates were always present, alongside qatayef stuffed with nuts and drizzled with syrup. We dipped warm bread in za'atar and olive oil, spread creamy labneh or sweet halva atop soft taboon bread, and washed it all down with sweet tea infused with fresh mint. Summer brought fresh figs, juicy watermelon, prickly pears, grapes bursting with sweetness. Our grills smoked with various kinds of meats.

Those delicious mixed grills are no longer within reach.

Before the genocide, roughly 550 trucks brought supplies into Gaza every day — even then, the city and the entire Gaza Strip were already under siege. As I write this in September

2025, relief activist Bassem Al-Batta estimates Gaza would need about 1,000 trucks daily to cover basic necessities, yet only a few hundred have entered over the past two years. 90% of the territory's food warehouses have been destroyed by bombing. Fresh meat and vegetables have not arrived for months. Malnutrition grips 90% of the population, and more than 90 people have already died of starvation.

In Gaza, food has become a weapon. What was once within reach is now unattainable. I long for a golden pie.

Simply staying alive has become an act of resistance. Not long ago, you could buy a tin of sardines for one shekel; it now sells for 30. Two shekels of fava beans cost 25. Two ears of corn, once three shekels, are 15 now. Three shekels was once enough for a kilo of sugar; today, 100 grams goes for 130 shekels. Yeast packets are 100 shekels.

Olive oil, even locally produced brands, is obscenely expensive at 300 shekels a liter; it used to be 35. I yearn for the simple pleasure of a Snickers bar; this one-shekel treat has become a 50-shekels luxury item. We buy eggs one at a time and single cloves of garlic.

Even these foods are not consistently available. Most of them disappear from the shelves for days, or even weeks, at a time. In many cases, people stand in long lines only to return home empty-handed. Even with enough money, there is no guarantee the item you need will be there. Scarcity has become just as brutal as cost. Hunger in Gaza is not only about unaffordable prices; it's about the near-total absence of food itself.

This isn't inflation. It is starvation by design. Palestinians are being priced out of their own survival. But the most impossible price? Human life. People run from store to store, chasing basic items, only to be told their money is too old, too crumpled, or too worthless to be accepted. Children wait in line for food that never arrives. The markets are graveyards of empty shelves. Families must choose between food and medicine, water or baby formula. And even in death, dignity is priced beyond reach. Graves cost 900 shekels.

Life has come to a standstill. There are no jobs, no salaries, no functioning economy. Even those who find work — cutting hair, setting up street stalls — barely make 20 shekels a day. That isn't a wage. It's an insult.

I watched a video that didn't just break my heart; it hollowed it. A man stood beneath a bruised sky, holding a bottle of water. His voice trembled — not from weakness, but from the weight of hunger.

"Flour is 80 shekels," he said. "I make 20 shekels selling water. What am I supposed to buy with that? I haven't eaten in two days." Then came the part I can't un-see. He lifted his shirt and pointed to the emptiness beneath his ribs. "Look," he said, "there's nothing left." His stomach was flat like a warning.

This isn't just his story.

It's all of ours.

Let history bear witness: nearly 200 countries failed to deliver aid to Gaza, failed to stop the bombs, failed to end the genocide. We will remember who turned famine into a weapon, who stood silent while we fought to survive.

Hunger gnaws at people who once argued over who would host the weary traveler or the distant stranger. It settles in the homes of neighbors who, without hesitation, opened their doors and hearts to anyone passing by, inviting them for a shared cup of tea. Hunger ties the hands of those who laid out plates of joy and comfort in the streets, feeding needy souls and wayfarers alike — never turning away a hungry guest.

Our lives were full of pride and dignity. All the videos you're seeing these days do not represent the people of Gaza. Famine does not resemble us at all.

In Gaza, we were not always starving.

6

WE LAUGHED LOUDER THAN HUNGER

There was panla in the pot again. Red oil & time.
The fish already falling apart like a memory.
My grandmother, old fingers flicking salt, stirring ache
into the broth like she was coaxing the ancestors to eat.
My grandmother's hands are gods. They roll the amala
like thunder kneading the clouds. We used to sit on the floor,
bellies first, laughter shaking the fish bones.
The soup smelled of before. Of you — squatting beside me,
amala soft between fingers, our bellies full of laughter.
We were small then. Our laughter louder than the hunger.
The amala split evenly between us & you always took the
softest piece.
You said the soup tasted better if Grandma made it with
her eyes closed.
I didn't understand what you meant until she cooked again
after you died
& didn't taste the salt. Sickness came. Then the silence.
Now every meal is a séance. I open the lid. Steam kisses
my face,
a ghost rehearsing your return. Now whenever I eat, I
check for you first:
in the steam, in the fold of the fish, in the oil that clings
to my throat.
Now, the laughter lives in the oil. It sizzles but does not rise.
You died too young;
a girl undone by illness no leaf could cure. Since then, panla
has been a wound.
I eat slowly, not for taste, but for remembrance. Because
what is culture
but the stories we fold into a meal? & what is mourning if
not the slow chewing
of memory when the body is already full? You are not in
the grave. You are in the bowl.
Each time I swallow, I call your name. I eat. & the grief
eats me back.

I eat my cousin every time I swallow. Her voice, fried in memory, crusted
on the skin of the panla. I dip. I chew. I cry like an open
pot. My body remembers you.
Not in words but in salt, in pepper, in the way I finish too
fast, as if joy will disappear
if I pause too long. The fish looks at me with a mouth full
of goodbye.

8

CUCUMBER SALAD

1.
You sat across from me
The bar was buzzing
Next to us the dinner party talked of the war in Gaza
We looked at each other heavy eyed
Being gay is the best thing to ever happen to me
That's what you said
Your hands were free
Your eyes activated turquoise
I know what you mean
We ordered crushed cucumber salad
The bright violin of green
And the giggle of delight
This was my first time back in Texas since coming out
I felt untouchable walking down old suburban streets
The houses used to cave in here
But I rebuilt myself and in turn rebuilt this place
I took back what I wanted to keep for myself
Every bite fresh

2.
After everything I came back to your blue house
I laughed as I ran up the hill to your door
The house was warm
And I'm still reeling from your smile
You held me from behind as I stood in front of the sink
I'm wrapped up in everything that you are
I watched you smash cucumbers for our dinner
Laughed at the barbaric chop
The unclean lines
What are you doing I laughed
But I quietly remembered I'd had them before
The messiness holds more flavor
We are better breaking
Never meant for clean cuts

DICING IN THE DARK

Down there
somewhere
a knife knows
more than me,
but still I slice
by the sound
& shade,
onions like diamonds
in the dark, the bright
smell as peppers break
against the blade.

ROAD TRIPS

I remember our first road trip. You packed Cokes for you, club soda for me, and pork rinds to share, the open bag placed between us for easy snacking. Strangely compelling salty, crunchy morsels. It would be a while before I realized that they were called pork rinds not because it was a cute name for a new snack, but because they were made of actual pork, the skin of a pig. We hadn't known each other long. It wasn't my practice to lead with *I don't eat meat*. Not a common enticing ice breaker. Years later when I morphed from vegetarian to vegan, we were used to it, our differences. A mismatched pair of soulmates.

You took me on an adventure to sample biscuits all the way from Northern Virginia, where we lived, to North Carolina, your childhood home. A quest for the best, the perfect, the penultimate buttermilk biscuit. You found my culinary repertoire to be lacking. All that fine French and Northern Italian food I'd been raised on, and I knew nothing of biscuits. Apparently, I knew even less about barbecued pork. You said the only worth eating was North Carolina barbecue.

You fed me boiled peanuts, pronounced *balled*, from side-of-the-highway gas station convenience stores. Spooned into Styrofoam cups out of crockpots, held for hours in hot, murky brine, they rendered our lips bright red, our fingers swollen like sausages. But, damn, they were good.

You made grits for the kids with salt and pepper. On holidays, there was your famous cheeseball — a package of cream cheese mixed with a can of clams, a splash of Tabasco, piled onto Triscuits — and white bean salad on melba rounds — canned beans, chopped celery, and spring onions swimming happily in Newman's Own Classic Oil & Vinegar. You made Gastonia Shrimp — a bag of frozen shrimp smothered in a bottle of Catalina dressing, baked in the oven, finished with a last-minute broil to perfection.

You loved feeding people. Taking care of people. In spite of your ofttimes unrelenting sadness and loss and regret, you loved life.

I remember our last ride. When you called to say you were ill, I said I'm coming to get you. I don't know where we stopped, and for the first time ever, I have no idea what we ate. I only know that I was the driver, you in the passenger seat, all the way home. We took our time. There was no urgency. Time forever altered by an ominous inevitability, enveloping us, coloring our every thought, our every word, our every breath.

You taught this Yankee elitist vegan that barbecue is a noun. That grits is singular. That boiled peanuts are oddly delightful. That driving the speed limit can actually be relaxing. That unconditional love can show up in unexpected places. And that it's effortless. That decades can go by unannounced. That no one lives forever, no matter how much we need them to.

BABCIA TAUGHT ME HOW TO COOK POLISH

When she bent
over cooking pots
the small hunch in her back
aligned with the craftsman's curve
of her upper body,
moulded by lugging milk urns
on long poles
that blunt-cut
across the back of her neck
when she was twelve.
Her elbows were walnuts.
We gorged on her pierogi, hand-sculpted
into frilly half-moons,
garnet borsch, like pious wine,
and vanilla-scented babkas. Inhaled
the real raw bean complexity of home.
I knew where the cake tins lived
and that tea in bags was heresy.
I didn't know then, that every ritual
would sepia as image,
but neon as yearning echo

OLDER THAN UNCRUSTABLES

"Uncrustables are thirty years old." This was not supposed
to be a heart-stopping headline. If it was breaking news, it
should barely break the reader's stride. It is the sort of nugget
you expect to find between speculation on whether Matthew
McConaughey will grow his hair long again and a story of
how a whole town came together to save the salamanders. It is
palatable and inoffensive, much like an Uncrustable.

"Uncrustables are thirty years old." My hand flew to my heart,
and my cheeks flushed with strawberries. I felt the need to sit
down. I realized I was already sitting down.

Uncrustables are dumplings playing dress-up as sandwiches.
These dimpled dough bean bags contain one dollop of jam. They
are mass produced by Smucker's. They are as round as the moon.
There are no seeds. There are, critically, no crusts. An Uncrustable has no beginning and no end. They are the self-contained
sacrament of the after-school snack. They do not need to be
toasted. They do not actually expire. If you put them in a fire, I
do not think they would burn. I think they are superb.

I thought they were here before me. When I was a child, I ate
as a child. Now that I am a child with grey roots, I am glad
they persist. No matter how old I get, Uncrustables will always
be older. I give them a little nod in the grocery store. They
smile back with all their dimples. Some grapes grow up to fill a
chalice, and some hide inside Uncrustables. There isn't one way.
There is ample time to find your stomping ground.

But if Uncrustables were thirty years old, I was older than I
knew. I could have sworn they were here when I was five, but
memory is an imp who will take your lunch even if your name
is on it. I could have babysat Uncrustables.

"Uncrustables are thirty years old." If that was the case, I
was no longer uncrustable. It should not have been a shock. I
look like I get excited about tips for stain removal. There are

conflicting reports from the corners of my eyes and the neon laces on my sneakers. My face and my spirit engage in hand-to-hand combat, until they both get winded and sit down to watch HGTV. I count blessings and carbohydrates.

"Uncrustables are thirty years old." There is nothing I can do about it. I will pick up a box, then visit the bread on the Final Sale rack. There is still life in the gnarly challah and bulbous brioche. The baguette has an exoskeleton, but its heart is soft. I will redeem the club rolls. Someone made them by hand, so they are imperfect. It is not too late for transfiguration. Bread pudding is possible. I will throw in a handful of strawberries.

15

SPAM MUSUBI: AN INTERNMENT CAMP FOOD

Some people say grass lawns mimic owning enough
estate to flaunt not needing to grow your own food.
Some people name human meat *long pig*, and I wonder
where the similarity lives: in the body or in the tongue.
Some people reserve white rice for the wealthy
and the colonized, but I say I can lose
some things like teeth filed sharp to tear and tattoos
to count heads, but leave me ghosts to remember,
even if it tastes like incarceration. Let me have
the consistent hum of white rice like a baseline
and a grasp, the slicing tin lids and salty humanness
of SPAM, and seaweed skin holding it together,
like how the ocean once encircled islands
before ancestors, money, and land locked us here.

16

THE WINTER FEAST

What winter lacks, as anyone will tell you, is good tomatoes. Also: sunlight, non-eggnog-related cheer, all other pleasing produce. This is maybe unfair to the crucifers, but who's ever been excited about a cabbage? And, more to the point, felt excited about it again, two days later? Yes, there is citrus, but excepting the occasional fragrant pomelo or impossibly-potent kumquat, there's something goody-goody about these fruits, a tang of the dutiful as we use them to prevent scurvy or pretend to ward off the common cold.

What winter does have in abundance is sadness, the glum sense of getting by, making do, a Sunday-night feel that lasts for months until it miraculously dissolves in an April sky that's bright well after it seemingly should be otherwise.

Sadness in winter is like truffle salt on bar snacks: in New York, anyway, inevitable, so any question about its specific appeal is irrelevant. Though hardly anything tangible gets made here any more, the city is still an unending producer of metaphor, memory and existential rhyme, which in winter becomes more obvious as other distractions fade. The sidewalk divots hold water, unevaporated, for days after a storm, reminding me of the leftovers my grandmother, Helen, brought home when she was still well enough to leave her apartment for a meal on a less-than-special occasion. She'd exclaim at each hamburger, each bowl of soup, or Turkish dumplings set before her, "Oh, have you ever seen such a portion?" as if her inability to finish stemmed solely from a cook's miscalculation. And I'd cringe each time, embarrassed by this old lady who couldn't tell how loud she was, who acted as if she'd never eaten at a restaurant and had no idea what to expect. I'd roll my eyes at waiters and at the meal's end would just barely stop myself from saying nobody takes home half a burger, a pile of French fries, not to a fridge already full of mummified soups and flat ginger ale.

Did she ever see me do this? I was sure not. I was always sure when it came to Helen, confident I saw the whole of things

she only grasped in fragments. "It's on me," she'd announce
at brunch, at dinner, as if any other arrangement had been
proposed. It's only now that I wonder whether this was her way
of suggesting that, for once, I could at least offer to pay.

Things linger in winter; there's less to hide them, and to haul
them off. But maybe that's not right, one of those declarations
that feels profound and so doesn't have to be examined. The
Turkish restaurant we went to is still there; the greasy spoon,
the only place I ever saw her eat a burger, is gone, and Helen
is gone too. My grandmother, who died in winter, really had
nothing to do with rainstorms or sidewalk depressions; the
only connection between these things is me, and I'm not sure of
my own reliability.

Smoke, anyway, does linger in winter air, distinct and sharp as
it never is during baked summer. You only occasionally smell
the smoke of roasting chestnuts now, but it scatters through my
parents' and grandparents' city memories, mixed in with Jewish
Harlem and skating dates, organ grinders' monkeys and the
idea of Canarsie as the very edge of the planet. I recall eating
just a single paper cone of chestnuts when I was a boy; they were
tough and grotty, burnt pebbles I could in no way associate
with what I'd heard. I did my best, while my father grumbled
about how much they'd cost.

I've had chestnuts since and I enjoy them but they're just
chestnuts, not memories, not a trip to Central Park or a stupid
song I know all the words to. Things will just be things if we
let them, but then there's nothing in them for us. Maybe that's
why it's so hard to find chestnuts now: they're just an ashy-sweet
mouthful, hardly any sustenance at all, and not a candle to a
chocolate bar.

You still smell pine everywhere, though, for at least some
of winter, when after Thanksgiving unimpressed men from
Quebec and Pennsylvania appear with their bound clusters of

freshly-cut trees. Years ago, a date and I drunkenly searched for pine nuts among these bundles, though we wouldn't have recognized any if we found them. We kissed for the first time in this improvised forest, because it was something toward which we'd been advancing all night, and because our rustlings had woken the tree-seller, who turned on the light in his trailer. Kissing was a way to demonstrate our innocence.

Her breath tasted wonderfully fresh even though we'd been drinking the same poor whiskey in the same dirty bar. This seemed like magic to me then and now seems like gum. I'd met her online, a nice Jewish girl who didn't love me and I didn't love, but before whom I nonetheless managed to embarrass myself a few weeks later. I was still figuring things out then, though to say this implies that there came a time when I stopped figuring things out.

Walking now with the nice Jewish girl I do love, with whom I've lived for years, I think of the recent discovery, astonishing but intuitive, that we smell not only with our noses but most of our organs. What, I wonder, do the tree-sellers' insides make of all this, how do their lungs and livers understand the new world they've been tossed into, of bus fumes and the steam from artisanal lattes? What is my own body considering, at the familiar annual scent of sap?

In January, of course, the Christmas trees reappear singly, dried but still pungent, to be chipped and otherwise vanished. This hauling away is another winter fragment of emotion, sad because decay is sad, because memory is sad and also harder to ignore when everyone is wearing black and buttoned up as if in practice for a funeral, when we ourselves become only memory.

Except maybe that's bunk, because if things remaining and things departing, things recalled and things forgotten, all lead to the same place, what's the path? And everything I've said might not be accurate, anyway. Usually I remember things one way, but sometimes another, and occasionally not at all. The key difference between the home cook and the professional, any professional will tell you, is not skill but consistency. So what, really, am I cooking here?

It's easy to put together words if they're only words, but when they try to encompass even the sidewalk, they falter. There's enough sadness, though, without adding this failure to the list. And not just sadness; there's enough of everything, too much. Good tomatoes will return; some things won't. The city, as much as it wants to think otherwise, is part of the world. And the world, even with parts missing, is more than enough. This is how winter is, because this is how every season is. It cannot be anything other than a feast.

FRESH PICKED

Fresh summer days
ever-blue ribbons of sky
raspberries and cream
robust spheres burst red juice
my summer dreams
My cousins' farm
moist smelling hay hid secrets
mewling kittens tucked
where mom could watch
familiar tugs on udders cascaded milk
for all of us to lap
The kittens were known domain
Unlike the chasms, our city life
the mountainous hay
secured distances
from statuesque bovine calm
only ears flicked answers to flies' drones.
Down grassy hillocks we'd scramble
into raspberry cane forests
pluck their ruddy faces into bowls
later to be kissed by cream
and then our mouths
I still love raspberries and cream
nothing tastes fresher
than time suspended
past plucked anew

WATERMELON SEEDS

    Setting the first icy slice on my paper plate, my mother warned me
not to swallow watermelon seeds. A vine would sprout from my navel.
    For the rest of my life, all would ask only about the fruit sprung
from beneath my shirt, waiting for my curved, slender sentences as long
                    as the flourishing vine. All I know is this. A tough cord
of broad leaves burst from my belly. Flowers folded into fruit
and swelled with wet, pink flesh, sugar, and light, every one a world
                    within a smooth, striped rind in a green as deep as summer.
Each slick, black seed between sticky fingers was as ripe with promise
        as a period, all those flat, black dots, an ever-lengthening ellipsis
leading to a day I might speak of the mystery erupting from my guts.
                    All summer, I swallowed every seed.

22

WHERE GOD USED TO LIVE
In memory of my grandmother Sofia Guermazi Mallouli

Nan was a complex of arthritis and prayers.
She stowed God inside her pantry
and chewed more surahs[1] than bread crumbs.

« بسم الله » [2]
« بسم الله »
« بسم الله »

The words stained her tongue like turmeric powder.
Her paisley headscarf was large enough
to host all the homeless and hungry inside.
Every summer, my cousins would gather at Nan's,
searching for good food and God leftovers.
Pastries blended with the Quran;[3]
we never knew for sure which we were eating.
Nan pushed food into our plates
while her lips gummed the Adhan;[4]
the two tasks seemed equally sacred.
She would not be pleased until we walked with beanbags
instead of bellies.
"Eat it!"
"Finish that, now!"
"Don't make me come and feed you!"
We had to bloat or else,
bring shame and disappointment to the family.

When Nan fell ill, her tongue folded
like a sajjada[5] after worship hours.
The homeless lined up outside her scarf,
waiting for a silk hallway to roll out.

1   Chapters of the Quran.
2   Translates from Arabic to "In the name of God."
3   The holy book of Islam.
4   The Islamic call for prayer, recited from the minaret of a mosque.
5   Translates from Arabic to "prayer rug."

Her mouth became an empty temple,
and the prayers echoed and echoed,
in vain, inside.

Has God decided to move houses?
Where would men go for worship now?
We almost forgot what the Adhan sounded like
without the clatter of unfinished plates and blunt cutlery.
The Quran sounded to our ears
like raw dough tasted to the stomach.
This summer, my cousins will not be coming for visit.
God did not move houses —

Nan did.

FULL

It was only later, when I
noticed your beagle
resembled a coffee table
that I realized
you overfed me just
as you overfed her.
We were small things
in your charge. When did
you tip the scales from
nourishment to something
more sinister? A bid
for affection? A way
to keep death from the door?
Did it fill a hole
inside you to fill us up,
your coffee table dog,
your pudgy child.

25

BUON APPETITO

I'm sure you hear my heart pounding as we settle onto the benches. For thirty years, a five-course meal at Antonio's has been the backdrop for all our big news. Always this back corner booth, away from the noise of the long tables. Near enough to the kitchen to smell the crock of fresh garlic, but not so close to overhear the chef calling his sous idiota.

You proposed to me here, hiding the ring in my tiramisu. I told you I was pregnant here, both times the announcement poured from me before our water glasses had been filled. We celebrated your promotion to VP over osso bucco, planning how to spend the extra money as we sucked marrow from the bones. I'd drained three glasses of Barolo before I summoned the courage to share my cancer diagnosis. A year later we toasted its defeat with shots of limoncello on the house.

I choose tonight's order carefully.

Aperitivo: A sweet Negroni has been my latest obsession, but tonight a bitter Aperol Spritz seems a more fitting way to announce the dramatic return of my tumour. A twist of lime to sour what should have been my five-year remission celebration.

Antipasto: For me, a simple focaccia with balsamic. I turn away from your burrata, my stomach lurching as the ooze of fresh cheese and charred cherry tomatoes swimming in olive oil turns to a spreading, festering wound on the plate.

Primo: Spicy linguine arrabbiata camouflages the fire in my cheeks. I blame the crushed red pepper and white wine instead of the shame I feel that my body has failed me again.

Secondo: Italian wedding risotto for our twenty-fifth anniversary. We'll have to celebrate tonight. Chemo is going to cancel the Mediterranean cruise we had planned, like it ruined the party we'd painstakingly arranged for our twentieth.

Dolce: Affogato for two. Caffeine and sugar so we can stay awake until the wee hours. Drawing out this last evening before we are again consumed by doctors, therapy, cell counts, and surgery. Your hand reaches across the table, lacing cool fingers with my sweaty, trembling ones. I will pour my searing anger and scorching fear onto your sweet, steady belief that I will be ok.

With the last bite savoured and the espresso cups empty, we reluctantly stand. I cling to your arm as we exit, leaving the confession in our booth. You promise we'll be back soon to share more. Beneath the scar under my left breast, my heart is not convinced.

27

CANCOILLOTTE, [kãkəjət], "KON-KOY-OT"

I would love for you to come visit my family's place in Charentenay, a small French village in the département of Haute-Saône. The land of cancoillotte cheese.

Never heard of Haute-Saône? Not a lack in your geographical knowledge. It's in the eastern part of France, south of Alsace, east of Burgundy, west of Switzerland. Look it up on your preferred online map. Zoom in, yes, you are right, you've vaguely heard of the Jura and the Vosges areas before but look in the middle and here it is: Haute-Saône, a rural, landlocked, forested area short in touristic attractions. The main city, Vesoul, is mostly known for a Jacques Brel song in which he takes it as the epitome of the middle-of-nowhere *("T'as voulu voir Vesoul, et on a vu Vesoul")*. If you are French, you will know the song and feel like I told you to get on a train to Timbuktu, the place is *that* mythic. If you are not French, you will look at a map and *still* think that you are going to Burgundy, though I told you *several* times that you are not. The villages have emptied out, most industries left, the cafés closed, and the shops shuttered decades ago. This is my happy place, where my father's family roots are deeply anchored. A place I've known my entire life so that I cannot remember my first taste of cancoillotte, too young to form memories, I have always known the feeling of the cheese's pastiness, how it sticks to my palate, it's bland yet still somehow cheesy flavour. A childhood delight.

Never heard of cancoillotte? Not a gap in your foodie knowledge either. Barely anybody in France knows about it. It is a rindless, runny, regional cheese sold in 250-gram plastic tubs — think fondue in a pot. Cancoillotte makers dry and age curdled buttermilk before melting the pellets with a hefty dose of butter, garlic, and/or white wine to obtain a yellowish paste. You can also get aged pellets, called metton, and melt it yourself but most people don't bother anymore. My 94-year-old grandmother remembers how, when she was a girl, people would age the pellets in burlap bags at the bottom of their beds. I don't think she's pulling my leg, she's sharp and loves her cancoillotte. I never get a good result when I melt it myself, probably because I am shy with the butter. My father always told us that cancoillotte is the by-product of making comté, but that's a myth, cancoillotte makers purposedly produce it. He also liked to tell us that The Laughing Cow cheese was a by-product of comté — and that one is true. Comté is having its moment worldwide; coillotte remains obscure.

If you make it to Charentenay, you will sleep in one of the blond wood cottages with tall, pitched metal rooftops and large corner windows my father, inspired by trips to North America and his love for design, had up-and-coming architects draw-up. Two of the cottages have airy bedrooms, the third one is a kitchen and large living space. They are set on a grassy, rolling field lodged in-between a bend of the Saône River and its canal, upstream from a weir so that the river opens up right in front and you would think you're by an infinity-pool. The sound of the gushing river will engulf you. You'll wonder whether you'll be able to sleep with this constant rumbling. But you will soon forget about it, it will become white noise, and you will only notice it when looking at videos once back in the city. You can truly live in the moment there, your brain is too busy cancelling out the sound of rushing water to worry about anything. It's a meditative experience. I will take you to the best blackberry picking spots, we will go to cousins' orchards to gather *quetsche* and *mirabelle* plums, we will make jars and jars of jam. After dinner, we will sample the same fruits in their distilled version.

If you make it to Charentenay, you will not get to meet my father. He passed away from brain cancer after being sick for five years and about six months after I gave birth to my son, a week into the first COVID lock-down. I will be there, enjoying the place he dreamed up and built, though incapable of mourning him.

If you make it to Charentenay and want to get re-invited (and you will want to get re-invited), you will have to not only taste but appreciate cancoillotte. Don't worry, it's easy once you get over the texture. At lunch, we will serve it with bread and a green salad, at dinner we will instruct you to drizzle it on the warm potatoes we will have boiled to go with a *saucisse de Morteau* (a thick, local smoked sausage). My North American husband, knowing he will get an annoyed reaction out of me, will introduce you to cancoillotte as "French Cheese Whiz." I will promptly correct him, cancoillotte is an object of regional pride and bears a Protected Designation of Origin. But I promise my mother, despite her baking abilities, will not attempt the "Tropical Cancoillotte Cheesecake" recipe suggested on the cheese's official website.

30

If you make it to Charentenay, you will have known me for a while and know that I was diagnosed with a brain tumour a week before my father passed and I may have shared that I had to focus on my own survival and the care of my infant and could not dwell on his passing. He was gone, I had to (re)invent myself as a quarantining, cancer-stricken mother, and that was it. There was no room for fatherless in this new identity. You might also remark that my writing about cancoillotte five years later could be my own sticky way of grieving.

If you make it to Charentenay, you will see my son sneaking in spoonfuls of cancoillotte and me enjoying his glee. When he started eating solids, his father and I were in no emotional state to try baby led-weaning or clean up smooshed avocado. We could barely feed ourselves and relied on prepared baby food and pouches. I was not happy about my son's steady diet of prepared pasta Bolognese, but we settled for good enough. We were feeding him, he was eating. He was so young, in the fleeting memories he might have after my death, these meals would not be the feature, right?

My son made it to Charentenay for the first time the summer after I underwent six-weeks of chemo-radiation. That's when we found out he would gobble up anything that involved cancoillotte, so he got it on bread, pastas, any vegetables we were trying to introduce. It was one of his first words. When time came to fly back home to Toronto, we defied the Canadian customs rules and "imported" a tub in our checked bag as the stuff would never pass security in a carry-on. By the end of the summer, my mother had found, in one specific Haute-Saône supermarket, cancoillotte packaged in squeeze bottles — "*squizeur*" in French — and she brought a couple when she visited that fall. The stuff lasts much longer than in the tub as it is exposed to less air. We cram an average of four squizeurs in our luggage to take back to Toronto after our yearly summer visits. It's always a stressful time when we run out of our stash, and I am fairly certain my son is the only North American kid that has meltdowns over the absence of cancoillotte. This is a tantrum I don't mind; I am okay if he associates me with the sticky nothingness of cancoillotte. I want this food memory for him.

If you make it to Charentenay, you will know my story and you will eat cancoillotte.

THE JESUS PLATE

kept watch over us
in the small dining room just off
the kitchen

as we ate
so Jesus ate with his apostles
the Last Supper
we ate meatloaf
& white rice & green salad & orange
jello I wonder
what Jesus ate?
probably nothing I would have liked
as a kid
as a kid
nothing more I wanted than to hurry up
& eat so I could play
in the park — *Patsy! Patsy!*
until Mom called me home —
then Jesus
would watch tv with us
Friday nights our favorite show
Sanford & Son

TO HEAR MAMA TELL IT

"Get all you want, but eat all you get," Mama would always say. Though we were poor, Mama always had a generous attitude around food. We were never denied when we were hungry, like some of my friends. We were welcome to anything in the cabinets or the refrigerator between meals. Mama made feeding us good meals her first priority. She was an amazing southern cook. I never really understood her deep relationship to food until I learned this story from her.

To hear her tell it, as kids, she and her siblings did not act out by drinking, smoking, and — as the elders used to say — being fast. They had something totally else on their minds — or should I say stomachs? Mama and her four brothers and sisters: Doug (W.D.), Jannie Mae, Dorothy, and Pete had a grand plan when their parents, Wade (Mama's stepdad) and Katie, went to town in their horse-drawn wagon on Saturdays once a month. The children would pretend to be busy doing their chores but already had a plan to execute a delicious scheme. They would head to the front porch and wave their parents off. They would wave and wave until they saw the red dust fly. When they disappeared around the turn in the road, this is when the choreographed dance would occur.

Jannie Mae, the oldest sister, was the head chef. Everyone else was a sous chef. They followed her lead as she barked orders. She began by making batter for the pound cake. She knew the recipe by heart along with vanilla frosting to top the cake. She had to get it done first so she could put it in the icebox to cool — to ready it for the icing.

She would tell W.D. to go out to the yard and get a chicken and wring its neck. Swing it around and around. Pull the head off. Let it bleed out. Put the chicken in boiling water. Pluck the feathers clean off. Cut it into parts and soak it in salt water for a bit — until it was ready to put in a brown paper bag of salt, pepper, and flour. Shake, shake, and shake until it was all coated. Jannie Mae would then place piece by piece in the hot grease to fry hard on the woodstove. She made thickening (brown) gravy afterward from the drippings for the rice and homemade biscuits.

Dot would peel the sweet potatoes for the candied yams. Mama would go pick green beans out of the yard and get them ready to cook. They drew water in pails and carried it from the well. They made both lemonade and sweet tea. They came together as a culinary team. Chopping. Frying. Stirring. Boiling and baking.

When Mama described it to me, I could see it in my mind's eye as a well-choreographed dance. Pete was the baby boy; he did not do much but eat what was set in front of him. He was a big baby boy, and he loved to eat.

They all were built from know-how and make-a-way. When all the cooking was done, they sat together and ate — but not before someone said grace. Then, they'd partake. The trick was they had to eat everything, which was not a huge chore because between the five of them, they had to make sure all the scraps were gone. What they did not eat, they buried.

When I hear about this scenario, I find it both wondrous and sad. It reminds me of the humble beginnings from which I sprung. My Mama and my Aunts and Uncles rebelled as teenagers not with fight but with food.

I grew up poor the first twelve years of my life, but I did not know their kind of hunger — to have me dreaming of food and dreaming of ways to make a feast a reality. We always had food, even if it was only struggle food. There was always something to eat, even if it was only SPAM cooked like ham with pineapple rings or Vienna sausages. They dreamed food — of eating their fill. I am sure, because of the hard labor, their bodies always wanted more. They wanted full-course meals, not just on Sundays or holidays. Their growing bodies wanted the nourishment every day.

I envision the second act of their scheme was also a dance:
the cleaning. They knew how the steps went. The washing of
the dishes and the pots and pans. Someone threw a rag so the
other could wipe down the table and then the stove. Someone
took up the broom for sweeping the house. By that time, they
heard the wagon with its rickety wheels making its way back
down the road. The house was swept clean — even the yard was
swept. I bet there was sweat on all their brows. They must have
had some joy in pulling off their secret meal. The only clue was
the smiles that graced all their faces.

They all stood out on the porch to greet their Mama and
Daddy. To the query, "Did y'all get your chores done?"

Yes, Ma'am.

Yes, Sir.

I am sure it sounded like a song.

RESTAURANT BABY

"To want to own a restaurant can be a strange and terrible affliction."
— Anthony Bourdain

Part I: The Great Wall and Ricky Lee's

I never wanted to be like my parents. Lucky enough, they never wanted me to be like them either.

I'd like to say my family had dreams, but that would be a lie. I've heard rumors of their dreams but never confirmed. For Mama, that dream was to pursue a master's in education and open a daycare center. For Baba, my father, an international student at a small Ohio college, that dream was to get a steady office job with benefits, the whole nine-American-yards. Burdened by debt, fear, and thick Chinese accents, both wound up waiting tables for ten years post-graduation.

I won't even take a stab at my grandparents' dreams. Those are buried so deep I know unlocking them would break them. But it was my grandparents who had the shiny immigrant story. Po Po (Grandma) biked nine miles to the chocolate factory in Ohio winters without a lick of English. Gong Gong (Grandpa) traded in his white-collared shirt for a white tank with a pocket for cigarettes. He worked as a line cook, with other immigrants, at a local Chinese buffet. In six years' time, they saved and studied enough to open their own restaurant, The Great Wall. In another three years, they opened a second location. Gong Gong once was a top accountant at his firm in China. When closing out the cash registers, I cried as I watched his fingers glide on the abacus.

The Great Wall restaurant was the place where my parents met. It was where all my birthday parties were held, where every photo in the peel-and-stick albums was taken, a second home to me and my cousin. We rolled around on stacks of 50-pound rice bags and dreamed of desserts better than Jell-O and fruit. We folded the Chinese zodiac placemats into little origami shapes and groaned at 10 p.m. when Mama counted and recounted her tips.

The decor of choice for the back booths was scattered Kumon packets and workbooks from the Borders teachers' section. It didn't matter the time of year or how old we were, we had homework. Our entire family – two grandparents, their three children, and their children's spouses – waited tables and worked the kitchen. That was their job. Homework was our job; that homework was the key to all of our futures.

When I was born, Mama and Baba, each worked two serving jobs, totaling 130 hours a week. At one of the restaurants, Ricky Lee's, my father developed an archnemesis. Ricky Lee (always Ricky Lee, never just Ricky) was a skim-off-the-tips and yell-in-your-face-type boss. Baba wanted a corporate job. Ricky Lee carved a deep chip into Baba's shoulder, taunting him that he'd never amount to anything, never be more than the nonslip shoes worn down by thousands of hours pacing restaurant floors. I'd later remember him referring to Ricky Lee as a bastard. Trying to outrun that voice, my Baba opened two restaurants of his own. Both failed.

Part II: Mulligan's and Macaroni Grill and Taco Bell and La Pizzeria

At a Chinese buffet, the tips are not the same as your ordinary "American" chain restaurant. It's not as "nice" or good enough service to warrant 20%, compared to an Olive Garden or even Golden Corral. Ma and Ba quickly transitioned to standard American spots when I started kindergarten.

Mulligan's was a classic neighborhood beer joint with dim lighting and sticky tables. Ma was the top server. Super cute and polite, always accommodating. But at Macaroni Grill, my father was only given three tables per section. A smaller section meant management could keep an eye on his accent and temper (when people made fun of his accent).

I never saw them tired, although I didn't see them much with our opposite schedules. In elementary school, I was too young to feel embarrassed by their professions. My younger sister and I were proud to send our parents off to work at 4 p.m. every day. "万安，明天见!" I'd say. Followed by "Make good tips and some money! Love you, bye!" I told my sister that the Mandarin meant "Good night! See you tomorrow" because we'd be sleeping by the time they arrived home at midnight. I'd sometimes wake up to the sound of doors slamming and the smell of oil-seeped clothing when they returned home from work.

If shame came in brick form, middle school hit me with a ton of them. I felt fully responsible for my sister and started to question my place. As one of the few Asian Americans in a class of 500, I was pretty much always playing catch-up with social cues, pop culture references, and the difference between teasing and microaggressions. It took too long to understand that a gifted shirt with the text "Made in China" and the nickname "Duck Soup" were not cute.

At the same time, I started to resent my parents' career choices. My father took a job as Taco Bell manager. "I don't want to bring my friends to Taco Bell. No one cares about the free cinnamon twists," I'd say to myself.

The image is so clear to me: hard plastic swivel chairs bolted to the floors, cold metal bars corralling customers like livestock, and my dad smiling a closed-lip smile with a Taco Bell visor on. I secretly hoped none of my friends' parents would recognize him. A couple times, I had to sit there and do homework while waiting for my grandma to get off work across the street. After Gong Gong passed away, Po Po took a job at McDonald's. Her nametag said "Grandma," and she was employee of the month too many times to count. I was starting to learn what shame felt like.

During this period, both my parents waited tables at a local Italian empire, La Pizzeria. There, the money was great, the business local, and the coworkers like family. I loved "Nurse Mike" and "Kitchen Mike," Stacey, and all their other friends. Baba was "China Mike," of course. I thought La Pizzeria was such a safe place.

I knew the owner's daughter, Nella. She was only three years older than me but so much taller and poised. They were training her to be a manager at the restaurant. I really respected her and her thick eyeliner until she fired my parents.

The owners found out my parents were opening a restaurant, so the obvious choice was to send Nella. A sixteen-year-old who'd crashed her Porsche a month before fired my parents. And it felt like the whole school knew about it.

Part III: Canal Grille

In 2005, my parents opened up a humble American restaurant with a focus on seafood and steak. Their concept was to be the "fancy" spot in Canal Fulton, a small town with less than 4,000 residents. The local paper said it "looks like a retirement home, but the staff is nice." That didn't stop the customers from coming after baseball games and church and before prom and proposals. 20 years later, they've expanded to open a party room and a separate banquet hall, and they bought the entire commercial property where the restaurant sits. Take that, Ricky Lee.

I worked there from age 13 until I graduated high school, full time in the summers. I made a lot of money. I learned all the social skills. I made older folks tear up because I'd listen to their stories. I was yelled at by customers. I bit my tongue and learned to smile. I was sexually harassed by customers and coworkers.

When I turned 18, I was told I was a bitch who was going to ruin this country if I didn't vote for Mitt Romney. I ran away in tears, and Mama told me to go back and apologize. I don't blame her. My apologizing to Bob was the same as us staying open an extra hour every Sunday for a seven-person gun club, the same as taking the 20-person local acting troupe that only ordered fries with marinara and sundaes, the same as my slinging steak-on-a-stick to drunk Country Fest customers hitting on me at 15. Every customer and every dollar counted.

As a teenager, I learned lessons that could have waited. There were people who lied and stole. Others who would disappear due to drugs or gambling debts. I became friends with people who later betrayed me. One ex-employee sued my parents for false accusations of ageism and racism. It cost them $150,000 and two years. Another tried to set the restaurant on fire the day we left for a family vacation. He spray-painted death threats against my mom in red (for blood?). This 16-year-old was not happy with being fired. He had thrown dirty pans away instead of washing them.

Canal Grille brought less shame than the previous restaurants. I was proud to be associated with entrepreneurs unless they were compared to law partners and private physician practices. The resentment still existed. The restaurant and customers taking precedence over me — just another thing I'd learned and accepted. Ma and Ba working 80-hour work weeks was my reality. I didn't know if the business depended on it or they'd just prefer it over time with me.

Part IV: Sum Bar

My mother offered me $10,000 to not open my restaurant.

All that homework: wasted. All those lessons learned: trashed. After obtaining a shiny degree in chemical engineering, I made Ma and Ba's dream come true by getting one of those high-paying salaries with the retirement benefits. I did that for five years. The fear and emptiness the pandemic brought was not a unique experience. I thought about my family, purpose, and the unrelenting question: "Should I open a restaurant?"

My mother cried when I told her it was happening.

I was starved for human connection. That hunger became my first restaurant: Sum Bar. It's a purposeful place where people can gather fully. A dim sum restaurant primarily, run by a diverse staff in Greenville, South Carolina. I wanted to serve the food my family knows and loves unapologetically. Selling what we want to sell and not what we think the customers are willing to buy. Like many other restaurants, it's a place to belong, and, dare I say, to feel acceptance and joy.

Mama and Baba and Po Po and Gong Gong had shown me humanity through their work, their actions, their businesses. And going from full-time humanity to the corporate world killed me many times over. I'd much rather talk down a full-on disgruntled customer than respond to a passive-aggressive email. I'd rather come home sweaty at midnight than be painfully tired after a 4 p.m. meeting.

Knowing and working with the members on my team is my greatest pleasure. Every person at Sum Bar cares about others around them. They challenge me and teach me something every day. From the beginning, I've been clear about the mission: everyone deserves to be seen, heard, and celebrated. Despite being in the dangerous industry that is food and beverage, my team has shown what a healthy, safe, and respectful workplace can look like. Culture over everything.

Owning a restaurant is like knowing a book so well you no longer need to pick it up. You sometimes can't look at it for too long or you'll question everything. Your employees know the inner contents of the book, even write some of the chapters. Some customers just look at the cover and flip through the pages. They think they know the plot based on the Goodreads rating. They want you to change characters and the ending. They think they know what's best for you. Other customers (friends) reread the book over and over. They shove it in front of people's faces. They love and cherish the book like it's their own. And in a way it really is.

My mother thought she knew what was best for me when she tried to bribe me out of the restaurant business. One year after we opened, I thought to myself, "I did this for you, Mama." I wanted to show my parents how to be successful restaurant-owners without embarrassment or changing who you are. I'd prove that I could be efficient and put the people in my life over the business. They needed to see what a third-generation restaurant owner could look like. How I've succeeded with my fancy college degree and straight teeth and perfect English. What their thousands of working hours bought them.

One year after that admission, I realized I'd lied to myself back then. I thought I was self-aware. But it was that cute kind of self-awareness where you think you know the root of your fear but you're still dancing around it. I thought my "why" was to show them how I could do it without embarrassment. They never felt that! All the humiliation belonged to me and my projection. Ironically, being ashamed by your parents can be the most shameful thing.

This shame is not unique to me. Asian Americans I've met also carry this shame sometimes called guilt. Guilty for living? Guilty for not living for the right people? Do I live for them or myself? Do I follow through with their dreams or crack open my own?

My family has given me too much. Hours spent in kitchens and host stands to give me the freedom of choice. For me to find out I want to be just like them, spending hours in the kitchens and host stands. To heal my inner child is a privilege; to heal their inner child is ego-driven. Am I the spitting image of a first-generation American or what?

UNTIL THEY SHINE

The notebook is put away; where? I can picture it, yellowed, spattered, spiral-bound, flattened. Most of the pages are ripped out, probably used to keep track of Scrabble scores.

I'm moving things around to find the notebook because my grandmother's recipe for stuffed grape leaves will be the thing that reunites me with my cousin.

My grandmother wasn't even Armenian; she came from raucous, hearty French-Canadian stock. She and my grandfather met as young teens. He was dashing: soulful dark eyes, angular jaw, wavy hair, thin build. In photos, a cigarette always perches between his fingers or his lips. A teenage swagger that says he'll live forever, now that he's been saved by America.

A talented natural cook, when they married he made for her the Armenian food he grew up with. Tough to say who he learned from — probably his aunt, who raised him when his mother died at 22. Breads, pastries: meat-filled ones, sweet-filled ones, *paklava*, *choreg* flecked with nigella seeds, little meat- and herb-topped lemony pizzas called *lahmajun*. Buttery rice pilaf. Tabbouleh dashed onto store-bought cracker bread. Lamb kebabs sizzling on the fire grate in the yard.

And *sarma* — soft, unctuous grape leaves stuffed with rice and warming spices.

He turned his sorrow into love, for my grandmother, his two kids, and the life they built. He turned his sorrow into food, and taught my grandmother Armenian traditional cooking. She transcribed some of it in her sumptuous handwriting.

I uncover the notebook in a box at the bottom of a rarely opened closet. There's not much to it, but what's there is precious. It survived several decades of familial apathy toward cooking: the diet fads of the 80s, lo-fat this and lo-calorie that. Joyless food, the kind of food that eats *you*. Then years of neglect while I grew up, ate vegetarian and then vegan, and then was diagnosed with

43

celiac disease. Only after that tumult did I begin to appreciate the depth of what food can be, what food can mean.

Now, the notebook is beloved again.

My cousin and I have been emailing back and forth for weeks. He's turned out to be restrained and thoughtful, maybe a little dark. I hide my sentimental streak so I won't come off as kooky and overeager. We write about our Armenian heritage and how confusing it is, how the culture doesn't seem to have an entry point for those of us who are "less" Armenian, and who didn't grow up steeped in the traditions. But we also understand that in the long aftermath of the genocide, the recent erasure of Artsakh, and current/forever aggression towards main-state Armenia, there are bigger and ungainlier fish for the diaspora to fry.

So, our family recipes are as good an entry point as any. I photograph a few and email them to my cousin, just in time for his birthday.

Our cautious connection comes after a 20-year silence. What was all that time? Our grandparents died young; his father died young. The deaths instilled awkwardness; the relationship lost its ancestral order. Without it, talking didn't come as easily.

I have a massive, old grapevine in my backyard. Planted by my Italian former neighbors in the 1960s, it gets bigger and frizzier every year, spreading mostly unchecked into four different properties on my city block. My neighbors died years ago, and every spring I fear the new landlords are going to get sick of it and undertake the daunting task of ripping it out, changing the very substance of our shared land.

One day I will cry over this but not yet.

In the spring, the leaves are small, tender, a deep green. I snip a few dozen and bring them inside. I wash them, dry them, and lay them face down, cutting off their stems. I give them a quick blanch in hot water, then a cold rinse.

I briefly fear it's sacrilege to cook the filling (rice, salt, cinnamon, allspice, pepper, pine nuts, cayenne, parsley, golden raisins) in an Instant Pot, but there is little question that both grandparents would have been really into this device, had they lived long enough to know about it.

Now to roll the sarma. It's a pleasant, repetitive series of moves: Place a blanched leaf down, underside up, put a little filling in the middle, and roll it like a burrito. The contours of the leaf shape tell you exactly how to fold it. Get a wide, flat, low pan and put a few leaves on the bottom to prevent sticking. Now fill the pan with the sarma, add water, salt, and lemon juice, put a plate on top to weigh down the rolls, and simmer for longer than you think. The filling will expand in satisfying way, creating a delectable packed-full tension within each roll. Brush them with a little olive oil (the recipe demands: "until they shine"). Eat a few while you wait for them to cool. Save the rest in the fridge; they're traditionally served cold.

Someone left this ritual for me, and I'm observing it. I'll do it again next spring, as soon as the leaves are right.

I haven't heard from my cousin since I sent the recipes, now about a year ago. I don't know what that means. Maybe he thought our conversation had run its course. Maybe he put the recipes aside in wait of free time that never came. Maybe he was struck by unfamiliar emotions and couldn't even look at my grandmother's florid handwriting, or communicate with me about what we've lost — a connection to Armenian-ness that's both no big deal and haunting, dogging both of us.

I know he's right there and I can reach out again. Eventually, I will. There is so little left of us that I have to hold on to what I can.

Stuffed Grape leaves

3 cups	chopped onions
2/3 cup	olive oil
1 cup	boiling water
3/4 cup	long grain rice
2 teas	Salt
1/3 c	pine nuts
2 tbs	lemon juice
1/4 teas	cinnamon, allspice, pepper
Dash	of Cayenne
1/3 c	golden raisins

Saute onions in olive oil until light brown
Add boiling water Salt & pine nuts
Cover & Simmer 20 min until water is
absorbed. Mix in Spices, cayenne, parsley
& raisins, let stand 15 min. Roll into grape
leaves, Rinse leaves in hot water. Cut off
stems Place 3 leaves in bottom of pan to
prevent sticking. Make sarma's place in pan
put heavy plate (bottom side up) to keep them
in place. Cover Sarma's with water 1½ cups
lemon juice & 1 teas Salt and Simmer until
cooked (Brush with oil to make them Shine
cool in pan, then refridgerate (eaten cold)

TAMALE

I am feeding my wife a tamale in the dark
my wife who is breastfeeding our first child, Thea,
wide-eyed, well past her wake window
I am squeezing lemon on each piece before mounting it on the fork,
switching the fork to my non-dominant hand,
balancing it carefully to reach my wife's mouth,
my wife who is half asleep, my daughter who should be
this does not have to taste good - *life* does not
have to taste good.
It just has to happen like this.

A NICE WIFE SOMEDAY

When I was about fourteen, in 1969, I was serving my father and grandfather the oyster po' boys I'd made for their lunch, and my grandfather smiled and said, "You're going to make somebody a nice wife someday."

I smiled back until I registered the storm clouds gathering on my father's face. I mean, it sounded like a compliment? I'd known since I was about seven that I was going to grow up and get married, so what was the problem? Oh, yeah. That other thing I knew, that I was sure nobody else knew, that sometimes everybody seemed to know anyway, but was never talked about. Awkward.

48

Of course, I wasn't eating an oyster po' boy. Not me, no. Way too fattening, and my mother already had me on Weight Watchers with her and my Aunt Betty. I'd already learned that, if I was losing weight, I was good. If I wasn't, or Goddess help me, if I was gaining weight, I wasn't so good. I loved food, but love already seemed conditional, and food seemed to be inextricably tied to that.

Again, awkward. Being in Weight Watchers, I mean. It's not like anybody ever really knew what was going on in my mother's head, but Aunt Betty acted like it was totally normal for me to be there, and really, lots of the other girls at school seemed to be on it, but that was the thing that I thought nobody else knew?

That I was a girl?

I'd known I was a girl from the age of three, something that also came with the realization that I'd better keep my mouth shut about it. So, I was pretty good at work-arounds (not in all cases, though. I wasn't allowed to play the flute, for one thing, because "the flute is for girls." Yes, it's ridiculous, but I got nowhere with that argument).

Another rule: no girl toys. I was pretty sure that the Easy-Bake Oven was totally out of the question, and I was right. Even asking for it, just once, earned me a largely unwelcome flood of stereotypical boy stuff and parental demands for more boy behavior. I knew I had to tread lightly for a while.

I figured out pretty quickly, though, that helping out in the kitchen, even well beyond the usual doing-the-dishes and other normal kid chores, wasn't unwelcome. My mother's untreated mental illness, that we now recognize as severe bipolar disorder, meant that if the three of us kids couldn't cook, we often weren't going to eat. I couldn't have a toy oven, but I got to have the real one in the kitchen. There wasn't any room for a toy oven in the bedroom I shared with my brother anyway; my father's massive model train layout took up all the extra space.

When I was eleven, I somehow became obsessed with biscuits, and with all the myriad possibilities of flour, salt, baking powder, or soda. Biscuits, scones, pancakes, waffles, cobblers, dumplings, the basic dry proportions are still the same, and I always had a bin of my self-made mix ready to go; the differences lie in the amount (and type) of liquid, the shortening, and whether or not you add eggs and how. I even wrote letters about my personal mix to the food editors of the camping magazines my parents subscribed to, and they printed them.

Another thing that had come along when I was eleven, though, was Boy Scouts. My father had loved being in Boy Scouts and always regretted not working his way to Eagle Scout. There was no question that my older sister would go into Brownies and then Girl Scouts, and that I, in turn, would join Cub Scouts and then Boy Scouts when I was old enough. Both my parents volunteered on every level and on every local and regional advisory board. Of course, I wanted to follow my sister into Girl Scouts, but I got through the days.

On our local troop's campouts, I was often appreciated because I was prepared, as it were; knew how to cook; and how not to burn things even over a campfire. My sister, who had been on Girl Scout campouts, taught me how to make doughboys, long rolls of biscuit dough wrapped around a stick and baked over a campfire. They proved extremely popular.

Summer camp with the Boy Scouts was a completely different prospect. My local troop didn't usually go, so I was there on my own, part of what was known as "Provisional Troop #XX." Admittedly, there was usually cool stuff to learn, once I got past the first day or so. I mean, learning about wildlife from the truly strange nature counselor who often carried two fully-armed skunks on his shoulders? Whoa. But learning how to turn my basic biscuit mix and a can of peaches into peach cobbler, baked in a Dutch oven over a campfire? I'm in!

When even my grandfather felt comfortable calling me a girl, it's easy to see that any new situation with new people, like the first day of school, was always an anxious scramble; Boy Scout Camp was on a whole other level. Time was short. I needed to instantly build a defensive coalition with the other weirdo outcasts in the Provisional Troop (no Music Department here). More importantly, I needed to quickly identify and establish connection with at least one adult leader who needed a confidante in this ostensibly all-male environment, to afford protection while carefully avoiding the lurking predators.

Just as importantly, I needed to spot the bullies, who often came to camp in pairs or trios; once you were identified as an acceptable target early on in the week, it was usually inescapable for the duration. Pretty much everything was riding on the first night's dinner, but if I was gonna get to cooking class, I had to get through it. Stomach churning, anxiety to the max, I would walk with my troop-for-the week to the dining hall.

The menu for that dinner was always the same. Every year, every session, the first night's entrée was invariably Chef Boyardee canned ravioli. I didn't even need to see those big red #10 cans stacked outside the back door of the dining hall. The smell would hit me about a hundred feet out, and my stomach would announce its clear refusal to accept even a single pasty lump. Thankfully, there was usually plenty of bread to go with it, and even terrible bread — terrible bread thickly slathered in USDA surplus margarine — is still bread. I would grab a slice, slather appropriately, and go to work lobbying and networking.

A few years ago, I did some pro bono writing for local non-profits. One of those pieces was titled "Glimmers and Triggers," and was about keeping a list of things that can help pull you out of the darkness. Playlists, movies, books, foods. Of course, any such list is totally individualized.

Chef Boyardee was on the top of my trigger list. No matter how good I feel, no matter the setting or the company, just a whiff of canned ravioli on the stove, something that may well make lots and lots of people feel warm and comforted, and I'm anxious to the point of nausea.

But at my darkest, six decades later, tea and biscuits reliably make me feel better. I make the simplest biscuits most often, with oil, especially when the object is food now. Mix them up, roll them out and cut them, then bake them in a 425° oven or even in a frying pan until almost crispy on the top and bottom. Sometimes thicker and softer to stand up to butter and jam at breakfast, or thinner to give a hint of crunch with your stew or soup. I can have them on the table in 25 minutes from scratch, and now as then, the comfort is as much in the making as in the eating.

BAKER'S CHOCOLATE

You know it by heart,
but your heart is fickle.

Break four ounces unsweetened
baking chocolate, the thick,
hard kind pressed with score marks,
into a little pot. If your hands are weak,
place it on a cutting board, get out
the sharpened butcher knife, and chop.

Think about how your body was scored,
ready for breaking, ready for a shake,
a choke, a shove into the living room chair,
by your husband, your high school sweetheart
who didn't care for chocolate.

Turn the heat to medium, whatever
that means to you. Not too hot, not
too cool, the Goldilocks setting
on your kitchen range. If it's not a gas range,
more's the pity. Watch for the reddened circles.

Recall how the temperature of your home
rose and fell, soared and shattered,
depending on his temper. Watch
as the chocolate begins to sag.

Pour in six tablespoons of water
and then stir, be stirred by
this occasion of sin. You are preparing
something forbidden, a recipe created
back in the 50s, you think, a plan
some man in a test kitchen came up with
to put on the back of the box. They would be
tempted, he knew; those housewives
would make it and have to make it again
and again and again.

If Memory Serves

Women are so easily swayed. Women are so
reluctant to believe they have no control.

Add half a cup of white granulated sugar,
yes I know that's a lot, and keep stirring.
The chocolate and sugar and water
will respond, the dark, soupy mass will surrender
to the heat and your motions. Sprinkle in
a bit of salt. Your sin should be salty.

This is a sin you control, you think.
This is an agony you ask for.

Turn off the heat, but keep the pot
on the burner. Add some butter, two or three
pats. Wonder why they call them that.
Pat pat. Not a slap, not a slam, just a coax.
Keep stirring until it melts, and then add
a quarter teaspoon of real vanilla extract.
No matter the cost, make it real.

Remind yourself you are a good cook,
a fabulous one. This is your creativity,
this is the place where you run the machines,
you blast the heat, you knead the dough
with all your might.

Then look around. Make sure no one sees you.
Pour milk into a glass, bring the pot
to the table, place it on the beautiful trivet
your father made. Try not to remember
how hard it was to tell him, how hard it was
for him to understand what had happened
to your marriage. *Six beers a night
isn't so bad!* But it was twelve, although
he didn't act drunk until he brought out the scotch.

Not your dad, your husband. Your husband
poured himself some scotch and began to sway,
though he never fell over.

Lower a spoonful into the milk, watch it swirl,
put another spoonful in, or no, hold the pot
over the cup and scrape half the chocolate in.

Try it. Swoon. Try some more. When the glass
is empty, use a spatula to scrape the rest
from the pot into a jar with a lid. Lick
the spatula. Lick the spoon. Put the pot
to soak in the sink. Go back to the table
despite your best intentions. Unscrew the lid,
dip the spoon into the jar. Do it again. Do it
one more time. This is control. This is what
we call control, now that he's gone, now that
he's actually dead and cannot throw the jar
across the room, as you both watch
the chocolate run slowly down the refrigerator door,
like a river, or no, like a little creek,
running a bit and stopping. Remember
how you wanted to run over and save it.
You'd put so much into it.

Remember: this is a sin, but it is one
you provide yourself. He is not the one
calling you a sinner anymore.

Force yourself to close the jar
with its lid. Save it for next time.

Or, as you have done in the past,
carry it to the sink, scrape it all out,
run the water, turn on the disposal.

Good girl.

Now tell yourself not to buy any
baking chocolate again. The trial comes,
after all, in the store. You buy it and
then it calls to you from the cupboard.
You tell yourself that hurting your own body
is nothing like what he did.
This is your doing. This is, finally, all yours.

BRAVE CAKE

The first time: my mother only 50 years old, incurable cancer. Me, just 26 years old, exhausted and caregiving beyond my abilities. At dawn one early morning, I stood in her kitchen unsure what I could possibly salvage of the day ahead. Her dented cake pans, scarred from a thousand forks and passed down from her mother, gathered dust on a shelf. I brought them down, wiped them dry and began to bake, kneading together fresh butter and deep despair. White, chocolate, swirled, fruited, sugared cakes. Round, square, stacked cakes. Frosted in buttercream, shaken with powder, cracked with walnuts, or plain with cream cakes.

I carried still-warm slices upstairs to her on grandmother's china plates as the sun rose. No matter if she took a bite or not, whether the cake had risen or fallen, when we had nothing left to hope for, these cakes, baked early in the morning, made each day worthy.

The second time: 30 years later a virus spreads and death hovers on a global scale. I wander the house wrapped in three-day-old clothes, piles of pandemic shopping casting shadows in kitchen corners. Our streets are silent. We hoard flour then ourselves — one-by-one my adult children move back home, find a corner, get through the days numb and unmoored. One dawn, sleet sluicing down, I watch the weak sun rise on another day of quarantine when a memory scent of cake strikes through me.

Wait. This fight I know.

Minutes later I press a tattered card flat. Find the scarred and misshapen tins passed down from mother-to-daughter. Tie my apron tight. Not just any cake will do, no plastic-boxed gaudy store-bought excuse for cake. Instead, cake made from scratch: softened pale butter; toasted cane crystals; generous teaspoons of vanilla, almond, coffee; the tenuously-bound batter folded yellow with yolk, lightened by the new morning air.

That first Covid cake-of-the-day was a victorious Victorian sponge — sifted, macerated, whipped then lovingly layered, sandwiched with strawberry conserve and piled high with fresh cream. Tender crumb that dared death to take one step closer to my family. Later in the midnight kitchen, I forked cream, berry and perfectly sticky cake to my mouth and whispered *take that.*

We were isolated but not alone: I baked scones full of tiny currants on the off-cake days, turned out slabs of gingerbread, sparkling lemon cakes, dense vanilla puddings. Gloved up my hands to safely place still-warm packages on doorsteps wrapped in brown paper and tied with scraps of yarn.

At the beginning, my family ate blindly until one day, knocking spoons and whirring beaters, I heard from the doorway *what's today's cake, Mom* and I was thrown back 35 years to my mother's kitchen, facing the sunrise and her smile. I dug out the china plates and slid the old pans in to bake.

Baking may seem so trivial, so housewife, so kitchen wench. But when you can create a scent that warms hearts and gives life, who cares? My never-giving-up cakes — strong with love, fierce with flavor, laced with hope — beat back fear, one brave cake at a time.

BACON GREASE IS AN ESSENTIAL OIL

Essential oils have taken over the natural wellness market and medicine cabinets everywhere. I myself have contributed to said storm by spending copious amounts of money on serums and oils for my hair, skin, and all-round smelling-good-ness.

One day while dealing with some ashy ankles, the shimmer reminded me of the amber drippings of bacon. As it slid over my fingertips, I thought about how bacon grease is just as healing. I wondered why, though we seem to worship bacon these days, we don't talk about just how amazing its grease is. In my book, bacon grease is an essential oil.

Growing up in northeast Mississippi, I saw bacon drippings saved in cans near the stove. Drippings were an epicurean Swiss Army knife — an all-purpose lubricant, flavor enhancer, umami builder, moisturizer, and first-aid kit (to be applied on small cuts). Now bacon has been trendy for a while, the "it girl" on everything, in everything, and everywhere. Bacon ice cream, bacon vodka, bacon candy canes. Bacon grease — sometimes reviled for the scent that hung so persistently in your kitchen curtains — should be cherished as aromatherapy, an alchemy of nostalgia, and ancestral ritual. It deserves its own glow-up.

The boss of bacon grease is the Mason jar, the preeminent collector of this sumptuous, sweet fat. I love to see bacon drippings sloshing in the jar before it cools — clear and clarified. Micro-bacon bits congeal at the bottom as it settles and hardens. This strata of drippings is an excellent indicator of how far to dig your spoon (or clean fingers) before you get to the bottom where the bacon residue resides. But you really don't want the dregs of the drippings. Just the pure, uncut amber stuff.

Most often, the drippings — solidified into a thick, creamy sludge at room temperature — came in an upcycled Crisco can. This was back when Crisco came in a can, not the tub with the pop-off lid. The can needed to be close enough to add a spoonful here or there, but not so near that it would become a fire hazard. "Too close to the stove" was a highly subjective judgment. You could sometimes see telling signs of a grease fire on the backsplash behind the stove: a smutty brushstroke of soot and ash still lingering, long after the grease fire.

Now, if you were fancy, you'd get a store-bought grease "container" that looked like an oily sugar bowl, with a cover. These were … cute, discreet, and fit into the *Better Homes & Gardens*-esque "nice person with the nice kitchen" aesthetic.

You knew what was hidden inside the canister. But why hide? The concealment of the grease always felt like shame, like you didn't want folks to know that you saved drippings. Rural sensibilities were a daily practice in the small town where I grew up. Reusing, conserving, and mindfulness were always common, but those who didn't grow up with these ideals looked down upon saving something so paltry; our social "betters" deemed this good stuff evidence you could not afford to buy lard and were uncultured.

Where I come from, clean drippings indicated more than your class background but really how you kept your kitchen. This saving, the meticulous procuring of the divine drippings, is as simple as just pouring or dumping hot grease in a can. But mise en place, a French culinary term that means "everything in its place," is a good practice of keeping things orderly, efficient, and neat.

I feel none of that bacon grease shame, for I know how to run a kitchen and I also know that the shame is about disrespecting the people who have prepared it. I've always revered bacon grease and the hands that prepared it. Those hands slathered in Vaseline, cocoa butter and Avon lotion, belonged to the women of my childhood. Rural Southern Black women who panned cornbread and fried simply-seasoned chicken, well-fed and tasty, with lard and some Crisco. They used the kitchen as a pharmacy and an altar and respite. Their food nourished visitors to their homes, and those who couldn't make it received warm, covered dishes to ease their pain or troubles. These women were the original Uber Eats, packing up meals and parcels of food to take on the road or just down the road to someone who needs celebration, tending to, or condolences. They'd quenelle (culinary school term for a fancy dollop) grease with their fingers while cooking a small pot of beans or a skillet of fried cabbage.

Bacon grease once coated my greedy-gut six-year-old mouth, when I decided the moth balls in Granddaddy's house looked just like gumballs from the candy machine at Sunflower's Grocery Store. A quick-acting tattletale cousin ran and told Grandma, who dug that mothball straight out of my mouth and swabbed my mouth with bacon-grease fingers. I'm not saying that mothball really would have killed me, but I'm here today. And I'm here to write about bacon grease's humble luxury, and my realization that "fat meat is greasy" (something that we country people say to indicate an obvious discovery or revelation). If you know, you know. But if you don't, bacon grease is a salve of miraculous wonder.

<u>The <u>holy</u> <u>trinity</u> of <u>bacon</u> grease <u>how-tos</u></u>
What you need: Have a can nearby to immediately transfer the grease to. You also need a dry kitchen towel, oven mitts or flour sack to pull the pan out of the oven or to hold the handle of a too-hot-to-hold skillet. The cooked bacon also needs something to absorb the excess drippings; a paper towel-lined plate or pan is fine.

1. DON'T MIX!!! Don't mix your meat grease. Bacon drippings are pork drippings. Fatback — a little hog jowl is fine — but to keep the bacon grease pristine, keep it porky and seperate. Keep a seperate can of utilitarian grease that may have fried some chicken, pork chops or vegetables... for refrying similiar crispy things. These are okay to mix. But don't even think about saving fish grease with ANY of these. That's just crazy talk.

2. STRAIN YOUR GREASE!!! Yeah, I mentioned bacon sediments, and that's ok. You won't get them all, but big bacon bits pieces can make your drippings rank over time. Bigger families and well seasoned cooks kitchens tend to use the drippings up fairly soon because they use the drippings as fast as they make them, usually within a matter of days. If drippings are not used within a few days, store in the refrigerator, where they can last up to six months, and reheat when needed.

And 3. NO BURNT GREASE!!! Dark and burnt-smelling bacon will produce dark and bitter grease. Your food will look dirty, taste acrid, and your family will wonder why that pretty cornbread smells burnt. Are the drippings too burnt and too far gone? If you have to wonder, they are.

Eyw

AFTER SUPPER

Amberman ground last season's buck with sage
and caraway and seasoned his meatloaf
with red pepper and shoots of green onion
after recipes as strict as antique
tales he built brand new each morning
or rain-soaked afternoon that left us
hungry as dusk in early April.

You know, boy, the real stories never happened,
tales you remember without seeing
never use the word yesterday,
but you heard them long after supper,
gravy growing cold in our plates
and the empty necks of brown bottles
filling spaces on the kitchen table.

62

THE SECRET OF LOUIE

I

For as long as anyone can remember, Louie's has been the Egg Cream King. Ask anyone who's lived in Brooklyn more than ten minutes. "You won't find a better egg cream anywhere," Louie's brags. "Go ahead. Hit Manhattan, the Bronx, Queens. Take the ferry to Staten Island. Find a place makes a better egg cream, put your answer in The Can, I'll give you a grand. That's right, a thousand bucks."

People try. They grab the strips of paper Louie puts on the counter, guess the secret ingredients, and chuck it in the can that's emptied every Sunday.

Someone wrote: "Junior's makes a pretty good egg cream."

Louie nodded. "Pretty good is second or third place." He has a secret formula. Big Davey's Dad got him to admit it. Exactly what's in it, he won't tell. People have tried.

"Come on, Louie. You know I won't tell nobody."

"That means you'll tell somebody; you got no self-control, Harry."

An enormous can the color of strawberry ice cream announces "LOUIE'S MAGIC MOMENTS." When Louie makes an egg cream, he dips his scoop into the can. Little Davey's Ma says he should dip the Brooklyn Bridge since there's nothing special in MAGIC MOMENTS.

Who knows? The special ingredients could be from the world-famous Fountain of Youth, forever lost in Florida's Everglades because that moron Ponce De Leon got goofy younger and younger. Drinking the water, he forgot where it was and forever screwed it for everyone. Ever since then, hordes of people schlepped through muck, seeking Paradise.

II

Ollie from Apartment 3C planned to get Louie's secret. He didn't do like the grownups do. "You can tell me, buddy," smiling. "We go back." But Louie stands his ground: "It's a secret. You know what 'secret' means? Secret means you don't tell. Not a syllable. That's how secrets stay secret."

Louie's secret ingredients aren't any old secret you can blab in a minute and next thing everybody for 50 blocks knows it. Louie's secret involves money. Kenny's Mom nods. Imagine what big chains would pay for Louie's secret. Representatives from Nestle's and Nathan's and Good Humor even once came by, stood by the jukebox and made pitches to Louie who listened, arms like a brick wall with an apron. Then he reached into his pocket, took a fistful of change, and played three songs: "That'll Be The Day," "You Talk Too Much," and "Leaving On My Mind."

Ollie from Apartment 3C thought he was so smart. He got an egg cream to go to analyze at home with his chemistry set. He tried to separate everything chemically. Whatever was left after seltzer, sugar, milk, and other stuff would be the secret ingredient. But he only burned his eyebrows and ruined his mom's electric eggbeater. He put popsicle sticks on the wires, figuring he'd turn on the eggbeater, swish it all around, and gravity or something would separate all the ingredients by weight. His little invention wasn't working so hot; he stuck a knife to go faster. Sparks and flame flew. Ollie, nervous, dropped the whole contraption and broke it. We told him when his mom and dad find out, he's the one who's gonna get swirled around since that eggbeater cost a bundle and his mom was nuts about it.

III

One afternoon, this man with a huge pale gray cowboy hat entered with two kids. Louie stood there, holding his towel in midair. The man stood smiling while Louie marveled. "Well, I'll be … is this who I think it is?"

"Think so."

"Mike?"

"Still my name."

"MIKE EWEN!"

"You gonna stand there showing me your tonsils, or you gonna fix three chocolate egg creams?"

Louie burst out laughing, ran over, shook hands, wet apron and all.

Mike Ewen had moved to Alaska. His construction company's doing not bad at all. Everyone said he was nuts, going to live where it snows forever. He says you can't believe Alaska's beauty. We check to see if he has furs or walrus teeth. He doesn't. He has a windbreaker and his ten-gallon cowboy hat. We gawk.

"Visiting your folks?"

"Yup. But I really came back for your egg creams. As long as I'm here, I'll have three corned beef sandwiches. Skip the cheese."

Later, Mike asks, "Ever think of moving out West? You could start a deli/diner in Anchorage. Make a fortune."

Louie scowls.

"What about my customers? Why make them suffer? How could I respect myself?"

Danny says Alaska is where Louie gets his secret ingredients. Mike Ewen mails them inside wild animal skins.

"There's no telling what's in our egg creams. Rare ice or minerals or mixture from North Pole magnetism fields that glow when the Northern Lights light up the whole state."

Big Davey shrugs. "I don't care what's in 'em. I glug them down."

Yeah. We all say that. We who would give their eyeteeth to know. We stare at Louie. We stare at the can. People hate REAL mysteries. People only like mysteries that get solved. We can't stand not to know.

Leaving Louie's, you picture the can. You wonder, "What IS it?"

It drives you nuts. Maybe that's the idea. Drum up business. People squint, figuring. Louie grins. Sometimes, in a real ha-ha-ha mood, folding those arms you could put two loaves of bread on, he smiles. "Guess."

WONDERLAND
Yazd, Iran, October 1971

Shortly after I arrived in Iran as a new bride, my husband, Ali,
and I made a pilgrimage to the ancient desert city of Yazd.
It was not to a mosque or that city's famous Zoroastrian fire
temple, but to a *shirini foroushi*, a pastry shop, *the* pastry shop,
the one by which all others were judged. The Haji Khalifeh
bakery had been a mainstay for desert travelers since 1916.
Everyone in Ali's family stopped there on their way to or from
Kerman, stocking up on the pastries that are an essential part
of Iranian hospitality, as important as religion, maybe even a
religion in itself.

When Westerners think of Iranian food, they think of kebabs,
colorful rice pilafs, or khoreshes — those braised stews with
artful combinations of meat, herbs, vegetables, and often fruit.
But to get to those delights at a traditional Iranian dinner
party, one must first have tea, fresh fruit, and *shirini*. And I do
mean *must have*. You can *ta'arof* a little, begging that you don't
want to cause any inconvenience. *Please, upon my children's
souls, I really shouldn't. Why did you go to so much trouble?
Your hand should not hurt.* But to refuse the host's repeated
ministrations is bad form — and, of course, the pastries are
ultimately irresistible.

When someone is the recipient of good fortune — a new job,
new baby, new house — it is his or her responsibility to give
shirini. *Shirini* can be shorthand for throwing a party or taking
friends to lunch, but it can just as easily mean bringing a box of
pastries for co-workers to enjoy in the break room.

Every good Iranian host has a massive supply of *shirini* on hand,
tucked away in tins in the pantry and arranged artfully on the
coffee table awaiting the inevitable drop-in guest. I was not a
good host. I had no coffee table, let alone *shirini*. Fresh out of
university in California, we had arrived in Tehran with two
suitcases each, mostly filled with books, and were dependent
upon the good graces of Ali's friends, who installed us in their
upstairs apartment and lent us a dining set and a bed. We had

67

little furniture, but we still had visitors. They perched on the unyielding dining room chairs and waited politely for the trays of *shirini* to appear while I scrounged frantically in the kitchen. I hadn't yet gotten into the rhythm of preparing for guests. I was little more than a guest myself.

I was still in guest mode on our way back to Tehran after spending a week meeting my new in-laws in Kerman. Ali had come home after six years in California with both a PhD and a new bride, so that week was one long progressive party, an endless tablecloth streaming from one living room carpet to another, with steaming platters of chicken in tomato-saffron sauce, mounds of saffron-scented rice, bowls of fragrant stews, yogurt with cucumbers or spinach, and plates of *tahdig*, the crispy rice at the bottom of the pot, placed conveniently near us because we were the guests of honor. Little children vied to sit next to us so they could be near the *tahdig*.

And of course, there was always *shirini*, mostly the delicate Yazdi versions, but often the hearty Kermani confection, *kolompeh*, a heavy, embossed cookie filled with ground dates and almonds. We had *shirini* with mid-morning tea, before lunch, in the afternoon with tea and melons, and before dinner. And when it was time to head back to Tehran, my sister-in-law prepared a tray for us to pass under to ensure our safety on our journey. It held a Koran, a glass of water, and *shirini*.

Winding through the tree-lined streets of Yazd in the dwindling light, we glimpsed traditional homes, surrounded by high walls and lush, fragrant gardens. Many of these homes had the distinctive Yazdi architectural feature, a *baadgir*, or wind catcher, a tall brick tower that captures the breezes and guides them down to a pool in the center of a stone floor, where they skim the water and infuse the thick walls with their coolness. These pools and gardens were fed by *qanaats*, a subterranean network of wells that channel water to the lower elevations. In such a cool shelter, on a hot summer day, a weary visitor might be treated to tea and melons and, of course, trays of *shirini*.

My brother-in-law, Ahmad, pulled up in front of the bakery, and we all got out, stretching our stiff legs. Tired and wobbly from the bumpy roads, we slowly made our way into the shop. As we opened the door, the warm, heavy scent of fresh pastry, a yeasty, heady mix of sugar, rosewater, almonds, and cardamom enveloped us.

The bearded, middle-aged owner beamed as the three of us entered the empty shop. He waved us in with a flourish and bowed slightly, his right hand on his heart. Happy at the prospect of business so late in the day, he was eager to make us feel at home.

"Welcome," he said. "I am at your service."

Ahmad explained our mission. "My brother, here, is just back from the United States with his American wife, and they want some of your very best *shirini* to take to Tehran."

The shop's bright fluorescent light bounced off the gleaming white tile walls and well-scrubbed mosaic floors. Neatly stacked pyramids of Yazdi specialties crowded the display cases: *Nan-e berenji*, rice cookies garnished with poppy seeds; *nan-e nokhodchi*, chickpea cookies; *sohan-e asali*, honey almond brittle; *toot*, mulberry-shaped candies; and *ghottab*, crescent-shaped cookies filled with ground walnuts.

There were also trays of *baqlava* — not the honey-coated, flaky Greek variety, but the dense, candy-like Yazdi version, thin layers of dough sandwiching a grainy paste of cardamom and ground walnuts, laced with rosewater syrup, dusted with pistachios, and cut into glistening diamond shapes.

We were sampling the wares when I glimpsed movement in the back room, a blur of white, and some laughter. Leaning closer, I saw that there were four men dressed in immaculate white uniforms and crocheted skull caps sitting on short stools arranged in a circle around a large tinned copper tray. On the tray was a shiny, taffy-like ring of white sugar paste. The men grasped the ring and pulled it back and forth among them, stretching it, their bodies rocking rhythmically to and fro, their cheeks turning rosy with the effort.

They noticed me looking at them and smiled at each other, amused that a foreigner would find this at all interesting.

"Go ahead, Khanum," the shopkeeper said. "You are welcome to watch."

"What are they doing?" I asked.

"They're making *pashmak*," he explained.

I had eaten *pashmak* in Tehran, but I had no idea how it was made. In the same family as spun sugar, or what the British call "fairy floss," its literal meaning is "little wool." The *pashmak* makers would work for hours this way, like jolly elves in some fairy tale, until the sugar reinvented itself. Its molecules rearranged, it was transformed from a slick, gooey mass to long, dry, flaky filaments — looking like fine, creamy white mohair yarn.

"Try some," insisted the shopkeeper, flaking off a sample from the large brick stashed in the display case and depositing it in my hand. When a brick of *pashmak* is liberated from its densely packed tin and pulled apart, it's like wisps of insulation material. I pinched some of the long strands between my fingers and put them in my mouth, where they melted magically.

Thirsty from all this sampling, I asked for some water. The proprietor disappeared into the back room and emerged with the largest glass of water I had ever seen — a fluted Picardy tumbler about 10 inches tall. The oversized glass only added to my sense that I had somehow fallen down a rabbit hole.

As he tied up our purchases with brown paper and string, the shopkeeper asked me where in the States I was from.

"Ah, Kaleeforniaaa," he said, nodding. "My son is a student in Chicago. Maybe you know him."

Like that enormous tumbler, his sense of scale was off, but there in that pristine shop, the rosy-cheeked men laboring happily in the back room, it was entirely possible that America could shrink to the size of Kerman or Yazd, where everybody seemed to be a few degrees of separation from everybody else.

Alas, we said, we did not know his son, but we wished him well in his studies.

We thanked the shopkeeper and gathered up our purchases, ready to return to Tehran, still with no coffee table but one step closer to being good hosts.

THE *SEARCHLIGHT* RECIPE BOOK

First copyright – 1931.

Newspaper clippings of Paul Harvey articles slid between the thick, yellowed pages.

A postcard dated 1969 and addressed to my mother before her last name was the same that mine used to be.

The Searchlight *Recipe Book*

The binding is almost off the black-and-red cover and the paper tabs denoting recipe categories are torn and ragged. It appears more novel than cookbook. There are no photos, and there are 40 recipes for the exact same meal and not one of them seems improved from the one before it.

Scrambled eggs. Hard-boiled eggs. Eggs with green peppers. Poached eggs. Poached eggs with tomato sauce. Coddled eggs. Eggs as a garnish. Six pages devoted to EGGS.

This was first my grandmother's cookbook.

And then it was my mother's.

And now it is mine.

I didn't actually inherit a love of cooking — or even a love of cookbooks — from my grandmother or from my mother either.

These were practical women. Women who were called upon by their families to provide in ways beyond the evening's sustenance. They were women who learned how to make do. Women who learned how to take minute rice and canned tomato sauce and fresh beef from a cow they butchered because its leg was broken and turn it into dinner. These were women who turned tuna and noodles into a casserole and you ate what was slapped on your Corningware plate, thank you very much.

"Who will get this cookbook next in our family, Momma?" my daughter London asked.

"I guess you'll have to take turns with it," I answered, hopeful that one day my children would want to pass around this archaic chunk of family history.

Currently *The* Searchlight *Recipe Book* sits on a shelf in my kitchen. A handmade shelf I constructed in fifth-grade shop class when fifth-grade shop class was a standard issue situation. The only thing of its kind I have ever made. This shelf has made it through three states and eight moves and multiple color iterations, currently a sunny yellow. A fifth-grade remnant from what feels sometimes like a leftover life. A perfect home for what this cookbook feels like too, like a leftover life.

It is so much more than an outdated cookbook that reminds the reader that appetizers should always be served with linen cocktail napkins.

Scratched and scrawled on blank pages and throughout the margins of this handheld antique are my grandmother's words.

Her thoughts.
Her hopes.
Her life.

In fading pencil and crooked cursive.

Recorded at Thanksgivings and birthdays and Christmases when this book was cracked open and food was offered and fellowship shared.

Probably a safer spot for her than a bound journal because there were no helping hands at the chrome-edged Formica kitchen table in a kitchen too small to even allow every side to pull a seat up to — one edge of the table forever jammed under the window.

Grandma, dressed in her house dress, a cotton thin robe with buttons down the front, her thick glasses, and a cotton ball wedged between the lens and her left eye. She had lost her vision in a bb gun accident when she was 13 walking home from school.

My grandmother, who was not a writer and who was not a great cook.

(She loved bacon and RC Colas — in fact, the empties stayed stacked on her back porch stoop, cases and cases that never made it to the recycling and when she passed away we had hundreds of RC Cola bottles to contend with.)

But what she had done — in between Ginger Ale Grapefruit Salad and Pineapple Pepper Salad — was to write scrawled words, almost illegible now.

She wrote about the people joining her at the table.
And the people who could not make it that year.

1957 – *Vonnie, Jack & Donnie Boy got home Dec. 17 for Christmas . . . it breaks my heart to see them leave.*

1967 – *I sure am lonely and miss Mama so much. Seldom a day goes by that I don't shed a few tears and want to talk with her.*

1972 – *Londa & Carl moved down here March 10, 1972. I never thought they'd leave N.Y. God does things in such a wonderful way!*

Valentine's Day 1976 - *What a sad time for me. Tom died so quick, I miss him so awful much, but I do thank God it was him and not me. I know I can do better without him than he could have done without me. I just need someone to talk to so bad.*

From 1955 to 1985.

30 years.

30 years of cooking and serving and writing and loving and losing and cooking and serving, repeated like the leftovers and the tomato sauce-based meals.

I don't think I have ever read my grandmother's words spread randomly throughout the pages without tears of my own, reading her words as she fed her own need for connection while feeding her family.

It's funny – how much my life looks like hers.

I'm a writer, too.
And also a subpar cook.

I think so much of my job as a mother is that of

Keeper.
Protector of Memories Past.

And so, I have pulled *The Searchlight* from the shelf before.

I have gathered my children around me when they were younger.

I have showed them photographs, weathered and worn, of my grandmother, their great-grandmother.

Mildred Elizabeth Lacy Norton

Of whom so many of them share a piece of her name.

And I have opened the cookbook.

Graham Cracker Cake.

"That's what we are going to make today," I told them, once upon a kitchen counter.

They happily smashed up an entire box of graham crackers.

They measured and poured and cracked eggs and mixed ingredients.

Like eating history.

Like being a part of all those years.

All those scratchy stories that helped to make me who I am and that will inevitably help to shape them into what they will be as well.

I add some scrawling of my own to the pages, right between the ingredients and the instructions.

I also tuck a few scraps of this and that into the pages, a few notes and memories of my own, where they will likely be discovered long after my turn as Keeper has passed.

One subpar cook to another.

One preparer of meals to the next recipe creators.

One history lesson to the subsequent history makers.

THANKS TO MY ESTRANGED MOTHER, I CAN'T FOLLOW A RECIPE

I learned to cook with hubris and reckless abandon from my estranged mother. I can't recall her ever using a recipe, and the only cookbook I can picture in our kitchen is the Irma S. Rombauer classic *Joy of Cooking*, which in hindsight seems more for adornment than for actual reference. Equally ingrained in my mind is an image of my mother's dog-eared copy of *The Artist's Way* by Julia Cameron resting on her nightstand. And it's somewhere between these two titles that her cooking philosophy laid.

Living in rural Minnesota, my family didn't dine out much, save for a church basement fish fry during Lent, some soggy room service French fries on the occasional hotel overnight in Fargo, North Dakota, or the annual indulgence of a funnel cake at the county fair. Which meant that most of our meals were eaten at home, and, in turn, most of those meals were prepared by my mother.

She was a renegade in the kitchen, partially out of necessity and partially out of desire. On the necessity side, because our stock-up grocery shopping trips to Sam's Club in Grand Forks, North Dakota, were infrequent. On the desire side, because that's just how she lived her life. And so I grew up witnessing her add a pinch of seasoning to a sauce based solely on taste, cook a casserole for an indeterminate amount of time based solely on appearance, and whip together a novel dish based solely on instinct — and what was in our pantry. A prime example: her locally famous (and aptly titled) dump muffins, which utilized whatever ingredients she saw fit to dump into a mixing bowl.

Even amidst our family dysfunction, our kitchen was a joyous place where experimentation and improvisation were highly encouraged. My mother was an artist in life and an artist in food. And although there were some rules in life, there were very few in food.

I wasn't aware that this was such a cavalier approach until I became an adult and someone asked me for a recipe. I'd learned to cook by estimation and approximation, often with great success. Which meant that each iteration of a given dish was slightly (and delightfully) different — and, in turn, somewhat difficult to replicate. So when I would receive such a request, I'd do my best, based on my memory of the specific meal I'd shared with that particular person, to recall which ingredients I'd used in what quantities, what vessel I'd indiscriminately utilized, and how long and at what temperature I'd cooked it.

I didn't realize the sophisticated and scientific nature of cooking until I began copy editing food content under acclaimed food writer Dara Moskowitz Grumdahl in my twenties. It was at that time that I learned, for instance, when and why one would employ glass bakeware instead of metal. How browning and caramelizing differ — and what in the hell the Maillard reaction is. And that there's a lovely French word, mirepoix, for that onion, carrot, and celery mixture that acts as the base for so many dishes.

My mother and I have been estranged for more than a decade. I have her to blame and to thank for many things, including the fact that I can't follow a recipe. It's both a blessing and a curse. On the one hand, I'm creative, resourceful, and at ease in the kitchen. On the other, I'll never be able to make the same meal twice. But it's when a half-baked (figuratively, not literally) dish using a hodgepodge of ingredients is a resounding success that I realize the great gift she gave me in teaching me the art of cooking.

CHALLAH

Two sticks of butter crackled in the saucepan on the stove as they melted down from solid to liquid. On the kitchen counter was a Pyrex measuring cup filled with two cups of warm water, a tablespoon plus of dry yeast sprinkled over the top, and a dusting of sugar over that. The yeast was coming to life as it reacted to the water, and the granules of sugar would help to speed up the reaction.

On the other side of the kitchen, in my baking corner, the KitchenAid mixer clanked around, mixing together three eggs, one-half cup sugar, and one tablespoon of salt.

I had awakened to a bright, sunny day and was out of bed by 6:30 am. It was Friday. Zack and Katie had both graduated from high school, and they no longer lived at home. There were no more school lunches to prepare nor carpools to drive. Katie was in college in Boulder, Colorado and Zack was working in Washington, D.C.

Though there was no need to rise so early, I liked this quiet and contemplative time of day. Following Friday night Shabbat services at temple that evening, we would be having dinner with friends, and I volunteered to make the challah for our meal.

The butter was melted and slightly cool, the yeast was bubbling up the sides of the measuring cup, and the eggs, sugar, and salt were well blended.

As the mixer continued to turn on low speed, I slowly poured the melted butter into the egg mixture, then the yeast and water. Now came the addition of flour. It had been years since I measured out how much flour to add to make the proper dough consistency. I did this strictly by feel and as the paddle in my yellow KitchenAid mixer turned rhythmically kneading the flour into the dough, my mind wandered.

In the nearly 40 years since I purchased the KitchenAid, it had never let me down. I bought the commercial-sized mixer from the Hobart Appliance factory when I was running a small catering business out of my home years before I was married. Before I owned it, I would make challah by hand, stirring the batter with a wooden spoon in a big mustard-colored porcelain bowl that had belonged to my Grandma Edna. Then I'd turn the dough out onto the marble countertop in my mother's kitchen and add flour as I kneaded the dough by hand before letting it rise and braiding it into individual loaves.

My sense of nostalgia for family tradition and continuity wants this story to be about Jewish tradition: the yellow bowl, my grandmothers, and how they taught me to make challah by hand as their mothers had taught them. But Grandma Edna didn't teach me how to make challah, nor did Grandma Rose. I learned how to bake challah from Sally Jackson, a Gentile who was not related to me.

Sally Jackson and I shared an apartment for one semester when we were students at the University of New Mexico in Albuquerque. I met her as a freshman when she lived across the hall from me in the dorms. Every night when we left the dining room following dinner, she would stop in the restroom off the main floor lobby and throw up her dinner into the toilet. In time, she would contribute something special to my life. Fortunately, this was not it.

By the time we moved off-campus into a little Southwestern-style stucco duplex, she was dating Gordon Hendrickson, a stoned-out hippie from Aruba, and she spent most of her time at his place. It was a mixed blessing to have the apartment to myself but often it was too quiet and lonely.

One afternoon I returned home from class, and, as I stepped into our apartment, I was overcome with the sweet aroma of freshly baked bread. Our apartment, sparsely decorated with cheap, mismatched furniture was suddenly inviting. The fragrant smell drifting in from the kitchen reminded me of home.

"Sally," I called out. "Anybody home?"

No one was home but as I walked into the kitchen I saw, sitting on the counter, a beautifully braided challah. It was still warm to the touch. Sally had left a note.

"Was hungry. Recipe made a lot. Gordon and I took some to his place. You can have the rest, Sally."

Sally Jackson was not Jewish. She was blonde-haired and blue-eyed and hailed from Connecticut. Undoubtedly, she had Jewish friends growing up, unlike my freshman roommate Joanne, who upon learning that I was Jewish discreetly looked for my horns. I wondered what challah meant to Sally. Was it anything more than to quell the hunger brought on by the midnight munchies and constant dope smoking? Where did she get the recipe? How did she know how to bake bread?

I pulled a piece of bread from the loaf as I took in the aroma. I thought about my parents and my three sisters standing together around our dining room table at home on Shabbat. On Friday nights, we recited the blessing over the candles together and then the blessing over the bread. My father would tear the first piece from the loaf and eat it himself. Then he would tear pieces one at a time for each member of our family. He gave them out in order of age, oldest to youngest. By the time he got to my baby sister, Judy, she would announce from her place at the table,

"Big piece, no crust."

So my dad would pull a large chunk of bread from the center of the loaf and give it to her. Then we'd take our places at the spacious dining room table for our family meal together. My dad sat at the head of the table while my mom, my sisters, and I all helped to serve and make the dinner special for Shabbat.

After one small taste of the bread, I knew that this challah sitting on the kitchen counter in Albuquerque, New Mexico baked by Sally Jackson the shiksa from Connecticut far surpassed any challah I'd ever tasted before. The texture was cake-like and the taste was buttery rich with a slight sweetness. I wanted the recipe.

Sally later told me that the recipe called "Jewish Egg Bread" came from a cookbook titled *Uncle John's Sourdough Recipes*. She didn't own the book but suggested that I look for a copy of it in our local bookstore on the main drag across the street from the university.

I went to the bookstore. As I pushed open the door, a little bell jingled announcing my entry. The smell of incense was powerful and Leonard Cohen sang "Hallelujah" in the background over the loudspeaker that piped music into the storefront. I wandered down the short cookbook aisle. Immediately, I spotted the title I was looking for on the shelf. It was not really a book but rather a little red pamphlet with a photograph of a bearded man in a plaid shirt seated at a table in a country kitchen. Uncle John looked like a backwoodsman just in from a morning of collecting sap from his grove of maple trees and was now ready to whip up a hearty pancake breakfast. I leafed through the pages until I found what I was looking for. Just as Sally had told me, there it was on page 34, Jewish Egg Bread. I didn't really want the whole pamphlet, so I discreetly took a pen and a piece of paper from my purse and copied the recipe out of the book. Then I replaced the pamphlet on the shelf and walked out of the bookstore as the overhead speaker broadcast The Band playing "Up on Cripple Creek."

***

I'd grown up on the Westside of Los Angeles. The air I breathed was upper middle class, liberal, and Jewish. My high school was small, private, and full of kids who were quirky, artsy, smart, and irreverent. They were all liberal and mostly Jewish. By the time I was considering where to go to college, I just wanted out. I wanted big. I wanted to blend in, and I wanted anonymity. The University of New Mexico didn't require students to write an essay as part of the application process. I applied there and got in.

Albuquerque is nestled in the high desert bordered to the east by the Sandia Mountains, which translates to Watermelon Mountains. In the evening, the mountain range turns red and the sky ignites with color as the setting sun drops down beyond the western horizon. Were the incoming freshman class of 1970, students who came from all corners of the United States, drawn to this awe-inspiring landscape or were they, like me, avoiding the need to write a college application essay? I was going to college because, given my upbringing, I never considered not going. I was not career-oriented, but getting a college education was a given having grown up on the Westside of LA. Just out of high school, I never thought to take any other path.

As freshmen at UNM, Sally Jackson made the social connections first and I tagged along. Those associations were mostly with longhaired dope-smoking college kids. Scraggly-haired Winston Prudhomme with his Southern drawl cruised around in a huge old Buick Riviera mostly wasted, though he still retained some decorum from his ingrained Southern manners; Randy Leger, half Native American, half Hispanic, was born and raised in New Mexico and had all the local connections. Bleary-eyed TS (his name was short for tennis shoes) had been a high school tennis champion, but these days he would have been hard-pressed to even *hold* a tennis racquet. And then there was a guy named Gideon from New Jersey. In my effort to hang out with Sally and the guys, I learned to exchange shots of tequila with all of them and go one better. This elevated my status temporarily. But there wasn't much more than that. I had escaped the confines of my close-knit community at home, but I was also lost and lonely in the high desert of New Mexico.

One day I ran into Gideon on campus and had a brief conversation with him. While speaking to him, I learned that he was Jewish. Gideon was the only Jewish person I'd met since coming to New Mexico. I realized that it was all the things that we didn't have to say to one another that had the most impact on me. Knowing that he was Jewish, I felt connected, understood, like family even though I barely knew the guy. Until the familiarity of living within my tribe had been removed, until I lived on a college campus as the "other," I never knew how important my Jewish identity was to me.

I dropped out of the University of New Mexico after my sophomore year and moved back to the Westside of Los Angeles to finish school at UCLA. I brought Uncle John's Jewish Egg Bread recipe with me. I shared it with the Sisterhood of my family's synagogue, and they published it in their temple cookbook. Throughout the years, I've taught many people how to bake challah in classes in my home and in synagogues. I still use Uncle John's recipe with only the slightest variation. I bake challah for my family and bring the extra loaves to share with our congregation on Shabbat. Those who have tasted it say it is the best in town and call me "The Challah Lady."

All these years later, I wish I could find Sally Jackson and thank her for the gift she unknowingly gave to me. She wasn't Jewish, but she helped me to recognize that I was.

B IS ALLERGIC TO SESAME

*"Is it not a strange fate that we should suffer so much fear and
doubt for so small a thing? So small a thing!" – Lord of the Rings*

B loves to say I'm *dramatic*; he says
this when I talk about things I love.
I ask him fairly often if he wants to borrow
my copy of *The Fellowship of the Ring*.
He never does. However, he has a "one ring"
sitting always on his bookcase, and
whenever I ask him if I can wear it,
he always says no.

B is allergic to sesame, but
half of his family doesn't believe that he is.
They must think I'm being *dramatic*.
But, his blood shows it, and on this stance, B
agrees with me. So, he has learned to question
every ingredient, and sometimes just not eat.

How hard is it to avoid sesame?
some people ask.
Harder than you think.
(Look at the back of your canister
of breadcrumbs ...)

When B was younger, he was also allergic to eggs.
So, I started making special pancakes without
egg, and they are still his favorite.
I made chocolate chip cookies replacing the egg
with banana — those are still my nephew's favorite.
And now, I bake my own Italian bread, so we don't
have to worry about seeds.

B carries his EpiPen in his pocket.
Can you believe a tiny sesame seed could hurt

my strong, powerful son, who is less than a year
away from obtaining his black belt in mixed martial arts;
who can shoot you down if he wanted to with his bow and
arrow —
Can you believe my husband and I argued about
where the phrase *"Open Sesame!"* comes from?

Has he not read *Ali Baba and the 40 Thieves?*
Has he not had to be as resourceful as Scheherazade?

B eats a lot of avocado, and I always remind him to
never give any to the dogs.
I hear him say to them, *I know, boys.*
But, you're allergic to avocado,
just like I'm allergic to sesame.

SPOONING

As I waited for the plane to carry me and my husband of two days to Rome, I buttered the roll on my dinner tray, looked out the window and bounced in my seat. I was excited. But it wasn't my recent marriage that had me giddy. Nor was it the honeymoon I knew would be filled with romantic strolls along twisting, cobble-stoned streets and midnight gondola rides.

It was the butter.

Because in addition to spending the last year making sure the band could play "Hava Nagila" and the photographer could get Dave to keep his eyes open, I had spent the year leading up to my wedding consumed with losing weight. Others may have fantasized about spending their lives with that one special person. I was daydreaming of walking down the aisle with just one chin.

Now I looked forward to walking the streets of Rome with my one-and-only.

Day 1
Speeding through the narrow one-way streets of Rome, our cab driver navigates around mopeds and dog walkers to safely deposit us on the corner of Via della Carrozze and Via Mario del Fiori at the Carriage Hotel, our home for the next four days. As the porter shows Dave the TV and mini bar, I flip through the folder on the desk. Tucked between a few sheets of stationery and a map of Rome is the menu for our free continental breakfast: bread, croissants, jam, butter, juice, hot chocolate. My mouth starts to water. Dave starts to unpack. I go to bed with thoughts of buttered rolls, non-Nutrasweetened hot chocolate, and whipped cream. Already I knew Italy would be a place where I could let my passions run wild.

Day 2 (Blackberry and tiramisu)
Dave and I are having dinner at Ristorante alla Rampa, around the corner from Piazza Di Spagna. At the base of the Spanish

Steps is the house in which John Keats died. At the top is a spectacular view of the city, and in between, throngs of tourists trying to get a look and a snapshot. The waiter brings us our first course: spinach gnochetta with gorgonzola for Dave and spaghetti with shrimp and tomatoes for me. The scent of basil fills the air, and I realize the dry, jarred spices I use at home are a poor excuse for the real thing. I vow never to buy them again. The pasta is firm and flavorful and nothing like the Mueller's I cook. I am suddenly disappointed that no one bought us the pasta maker from our registry. The waiter serves us lamb and sole for our second courses, and, even though I am satiated, we stop for gelato on the way back to the hotel. The sweet, pure flavors are orgasmic. I know that my trip to Italy will not be complete if I do not try each flavor at least once.

Day 3 (Chocolate and pistachio)
After arriving in Florence, we meet Jill and Eric at a café in Piazza Della Signoria. "You have to try their hot chocolate," Jill says. "It's like drinking chocolate syrup." I agree and commend Dave once again for choosing such a perfect place for our honeymoon. We take a bus to Impruneta, a small town just outside Florence where Jill's family has rented an 18th century villa. After Roberta gives us the grand tour and Arthur points out the shrapnel left behind from the Nazis, their cooks serve us Rosh Hashanah dinner, Italian style: Vegetable soup. Mozzarella and tomatoes. Salad. Pasta with chicken, mushrooms, and olives. Salmon, potatoes, brussels sprouts. I think of my mother who had no doubt prepared an equally overwhelming menu for the Jewish New Year my family is celebrating without me: freshly baked challah, chicken soup, salad, Cornish game hen and roast meat, orzo, string beans with almonds. Dave and I don't know Jill's family very well, but the atmosphere at the table is joyous and comfortable, and I feel as if I am home in Brooklyn. Maybe it's being with other Jews. Maybe it's being with other New Yorkers. Maybe it's just all this food.

Day 4

On a friend's recommendation, we make dinner reservations
at a little hole in the wall called Buca della Orafo. At last, we
would dine like real Italians — without menus in English or
busloads of tourists at the surrounding tables. We arrive for our
9:30 reservation on time. Five minutes go by. 10. The people
behind us in line are seated. The owner hasn't made eye contact
yet. "This has a soup guy feel," Dave whispers. "You know, from
Seinfeld…the Soup Nazi?" And even though the white-haired
gentleman running the restaurant didn't appear to be mean,
or crazy, his restaurant did seem to run on an unspoken set of
rules. Anywhere else I would have asked about our table.

But I feared ruining Dave's opportunity to dine on the Bistecca
al Kg (Florentine steak, sold by the kilo) and Funghi Trifolati
(Porcini mushrooms) he had been salivating for all day. They,
too, were recommended by our friend. Eventually, we are seated
at the end of a long banquet table. The room held no more than
50 people and its wood paneling and beaded curtains made it
feel as if we were dining in someone's rec room. Watching the
other customers bid farewell with a kiss or handshake for the
owner, I felt as if we were crashing a private party. But we soon
joined in the camaraderie; as we were served our steak, the
woman next to Dave commented on how good it looked. Dave
in turn offered her a piece and Carol from Seattle accepted.
As the three of us dined on a very large, very flavorful piece of
meat I tried in vain to imagine the same scene taking place back
in the States. I couldn't decide which was harder to picture:
sharing our meal with a complete stranger or allowing myself
the sinful pleasure of red meat.

Day 5 (Cream and tiramisu)

21 miles south of Florence is Siena, a walled city known for
its narrow streets, medieval gates, and gothic palaces. What
intrigues me the most are the beautiful bags of multi-colored
pasta sold in the local wine and cheese shops. Whether braided

89

in long strands or shaped like little hats, each individual piece
of pasta is an edible work of art, infused with a rainbow of
colors. I cannot resist buying two bags — one to cook and one
to display.

Day 6 (Peach, milk, and Mars candy bar)
It's been a week since we started our honeymoon and already,
I'm bored. For months, it was all I could think about — but
now it's as though I've gotten my fill and the excitement is gone.
Dave and I decide to break our routine and try something we've
never done before — have dinner at an Italian fast food place.
Kenny's Pizza features much more than pizza; Dave orders the
Cheese Kenny (cheeseburger) and I have the Chicken Nagghy
(chicken nuggets). Given that I have been abstinent for almost
a year, I relish every greasy bite. At 22,000 lire (about $15) for
both of us, it is the cheapest meal we have eaten since we arrived
in Italy, and that in itself is a turn-on for my frugal husband.

Day 7 (Chocolate chip)
For a week now I have been lusting after the meringue cookies
sold in every patisserie in the country. Finally, I give in to my
urges and buy a few. They taste wonderful. Not because they're
any different from the ones I can get back home from one of
the Detroit bakeries, but because for months I had deprived
myself of such pleasures. But now the wedding was over, and I
no longer felt compelled to watch what I eat. I take another bite
and savor my newfound freedom.

Day 8 (Chocolate and banana)
Venice is known for its hand-blown glass. And on our way to
dinner, we pass stores filled with colorful glass bowls, perfume
bottles, jewelry, and miniature animals. It seems there isn't
anything the talented glassblowers on the island of Murano
can't make. The bright colors and fanciful striped patterns make
the vases look like candy. Then again, maybe I'm just hungry.

Day 9 (Meringue and Gianduiotti chocolate)
On our flight home, I sit back in my seat, close my eyes, and reflect on the past 10 days. Staring at the Sistine Chapel. Feeding pigeons in San Marco. Finally finding, on our very last day, the meringue gelato I had been searching for since first arriving in Rome.

Our honeymoon was sweet, passionate, indulgent. The months before the wedding, I had denied myself tremendous pleasure. These past two weeks, I rediscovered it. In a hotel in Rome. In a restaurant in Florence. In the streets of Venice. And after two weeks straight of getting it whenever I wanted, I am returning home completely satisfied.

91

THE POTATO BALL SMUGGLERS

"These are the best potato balls your mom has ever made," my partner exclaimed. Mango sour chutney ran down their knuckles.

My Guyanese mom had just gotten back to the States from living abroad with a husband who isn't my father. Though she'd barely unpacked, she was already cooking for me and my siblings again. It had been a long time since I had eaten her food and secretly shared it with Alistair, the same time in which I've struggled to feed myself and find meaning in cooking again. It's a running gag between Alistair and me that my mom has never met them but they have met her dozens of times.

My partner is an Oklahoma-raised trans person whose relationship to food was scarce and creative, shaped by poverty and generational pain. In our time together, they've learned the balming impact of Caribbean food — and being fed food prepared by a loved one. They've developed a preference for my mom's dhal and roti and can distinguish the burnt-together spices that flavor her chana. What reigns supreme though, are her fried potato balls with mango sour chutney, a recipe my mother easily produces by the bucketload.

As a trained chef, I have never attempted this recipe. Just as my mother and partner have never eaten together. It's an intimate form of isolation. I'd only seen it before in cousins who lived in the dark parts of their homes, away from any relative who could discover their queerness.

When I first told my mother of my relationship, she removed herself from my life entirely. The idea of her youngest daughter not marrying a cis Muslim man sat bitter on her tongue. In my mom's mind — and in the Quran, as she so often reminds me — being queer is haram (forbidden) and an obscenity in the eyes of Allah. It renders useless all efforts to please God.

For the first two years of my relationship and for the first time in my life, my mom did not call or reach out to me. She sent no food, no signatures, or my favorites. It wasn't just a single container of food I'd receive; it was multiple bowls of meats and rice; a Ziploc of marinated chicken she reminds me to freeze as soon as I get home; a couple cans of beans; the occasional lip gloss or bra she found at the store and kept for me. In her language of care, these everyday gifts say that her children are the center of her universe.

Food is to my relationship with my mother as dialect is to language, a speech only the two of us know. Despite her conventionalities as a Muslim Guyanese woman, my mother was my first example of true sexuality and discipline in the kitchen. There was a breathless and seductive order to how she did things when cooking, one that I still try to replicate as a chef today, from butchering and marinating cuts of meat to who is served which piece and why. It was the kind of feral feminine energy that you could taste in her food. Deeply simmered, warm, and bountiful.

We share the work of being designated ritualists of tradition and dance smoothly around each other in the kitchen. My mother plans her life around the foods of occasion, and she taught me to do the same. Chicken curry on Sundays, pails of slaughtered mutton on Eid, tiny boxes filled with Guyanese sweets when a baby is born, beef and barley soup when someone is sick. These ceremonies give purpose to living and a way of life to spend your days.

Those places of such deep togetherness fractured the day I brought my partner home. The mind of my mouth and the mouth of my mind snapped. I became chronically aimless. My sense of taste, gone. My desire to eat, gone. The act itself of cooking became a threat. Wondering what pot to use would send me spiraling. I couldn't cook without leaving my body. I'd only come back when my brain registered that it had to continue moving despite knowing no one was going to care for us the way they care for the family's cis couples. Despite knowing, because knowing everything is now up to us. Ever so slowly, I'd leave the frozen state and the stiffened posture. My chest ached with melancholy. It was grief.

Today, the act of my mother cooking tethers us to what used to be, a home that was whole, not aching or privately breaking apart. But when Mom cooks now, she sees us kids as still young and malleable. Not adults living the paths we've chosen for ourselves and most definitely not My Very Trans and Queer Life with Alistair. Which to us is just our love story, two lives coming together, laughing through pain and building a future.

My mother can ignore this present and future love, tuck away knowledge that I am not the person she wishes me to be. I can sit with her at dinner and, over the table, try to prove to her that I have not changed. I thought that if I filled our conversation with the reminder that I, too, believe in Allah and family, she would see I'm the same person that she raised and, of all her children, the clearest reflection of her.

Still, my partner cannot join us in a meal. I have to believe that, despite all my mother has refused us, they have felt her warmth in braised curry beef, jars of chai spiced with too much star anise, and endless Tupperwares of rice. Trying to survive my mother's intolerance landed me in the arms of the family I am creating with my partner in our own kitchen. We cook for the occasions *we* herald as ceremony. We make ingredient lists and shop produce. We set our table with candles and two canvas napkins. We dish food onto vintage porcelain platters and assemble it romantically, primed for whomever might stop by and accept our invitations to linger and love.

YOUR HANDS LOOK DIFFERENT NOW

You watch your hands change under a meat slicer. They have more veins and they are larger now. You start to recognize your reflection in the deli bathroom. You hold your hands under the slicer and catch the cheese that falls. They feel the same, but your hands move faster. You flip eggs faster. You soak up the heat under the grill with ease now. You keep catching cheese and ham sliced as thin as possible for the customers at the deli.

Arguably, the biggest difference is treatment from the other side of the grill by deli folk, customers and staff alike. You are inexperienced. You are still inexperienced. Yet you are treated like you understand more. You are doing the same thing. You are slicing meat and flipping eggs for the classic NYC deli bacon, egg, and cheese sandwich.

You start to feel more comfortable. You can let your guard down now at night when a crowd comes in after a night of partying. You don't need to defend your skill as much. Drunk men nod at you with respect after you hand them a greasy bacon, egg, and cheese and ring them up for a slushie. You don't need to fear a lingering customer wandering the store. You have the same instinct. You feel the same gut-wrenching fear as you bleach down the slicer, wipe the counters, and shut the register late at night. You are alone still, but you are safer. Your masculinity is shielding you. They don't know anymore. You are seven months on testosterone. You watch your hands change. You can let your guard down and you keep flipping eggs.

In understanding gender, you grow a fixation on constant distraction. You find solace in the repetitive motions that, by nature, follow cooking. Only as your hands assemble the food are you able to unpack the intricacies of the effect gender has had on your life.

You think back to working with food full time for the first time. You ran the coffee counter inside of a larger restaurant, and you shucked oysters at the same restaurant across the way with your best friend. You picked up jobs together and got a lot more responsibility than you were necessarily qualified for, but, amid a pandemic and ongoing food labor shortages, they threw you in. You ran with it. You take the money slipped in your back pocket as your insides churn. You and your best friend keep laughing. You weaponize your femininity together. Do you despise it? Sort of, but using it gives you a leg up. You wink at male customers. You make them feel special. You let them talk. You let them start their mornings with the pretty girls at the coffee bar. They are still talking, you let them. You play the role so well you lose track of yourself. They are probably still talking.

You're at another breakfast joint now. You shorten your name. You live in between the binaries of the gender roles that gave you those same perks a few months prior. Things are different. You move cautiously and slowly. You don't want their discomfort to affect you. You sense their fear. You feel their confusion, or hatred, or discontent with your gender presentation.

You accidentally let the past in when you smile a little too comfortably at a male customer. It's a hot cup of coffee thrown back at you. They don't want your attention now. They do not want to be associated with whatever you are. You are not sure what you are. You have not been exposed to people like you before. You never struggled before in undressing yourself. In changing your presentation, it's not the immediate relief you expect, but a continual unlearning of the inescapable binaries you are between. You hear more hateful things escape the mouths of the men you work for. You keep creating new food. You assemble more complicated menus. You get to work with fresh produce you haven't been exposed to and learn to smoke meat for grit bowls. You focus on the food. In the chaos of a rush, you feel sane. You are living to understand now. You are unpacking a lifetime of misunderstanding.

More importantly, you can bite back now. You can earn respect from those you work for with consistency and time. You thrive on the consistency of schedule. You watch a bullet list of goals for the day get checked off, prepped, and sent out to customers. You watch a kitchen that looks destroyed become pristine and brand-new within the same nine hours. You get asked weird and inherently personal questions on your body. You don't know what you are aspiring to do. You are questioned. You ask yourself why you want so badly to be what you have despised for so long. Your relationships change. You feel limited in expressing the same joys of your femininity. You struggle in building connections. You are on edge in sharing yourself in fear of becoming predatory.

You hold your hands under the slicer and catch the cheese that falls. You are inexperienced. You are still inexperienced. You will continue to learn. You will bend between the binaries of your gender and use it to create. You will foster new relationships with authenticity. The trans experience has never been bound to cisnormative gender roles, but it has been challenging them for far longer than you have been here. To be trans is to unlearn every gendered experience you come across, and act with intention. You will no longer use your transness as a definition but to bridge the unexplainable in both identity and magic of food. You will with move with your food. You will work with your hands to learn. You will foster new relationships you have longed for. Food has been a vessel for transformation and creativity far longer than you. You will look at your hands and recognize them.

CERRADO (SURVIVAL) GUIDE

Welcome to the Cerrado (Survival) Guide,
where nothing is easy,
not even lunch.

Sidekick: Trust no yellow fruit.
That *pequi*?
Looks like sunshine. Smells like the entire city has been slow-
cooking desire and danger.
But one reckless bite and suddenly you're at the dentist,
Or worse.
explaining how you got a mouthful of spikes from something
your mom called a "delicacy."
And it was.
It is.
I'll die on this hill.
Perhaps I'll just die... full of spikes.
Villain: *Guairoba (Guariroba?).*
Bitter on purpose.
A botanical middle finger from the cerrado straight to your
taste buds.
It's like your grandmother's cooking with a built-in moral lesson:
Life is hard, darling. Swallow it anyway.
(And smile while you do it, or you'll get served twice)
Main Character: Feijoada.
Ah, the peace treaty and the battleground,
all in one simmering pot.
A culinary event so dramatic
it needs a full day's warning and three Tupperwares for leftovers.
There will be politics at the table.
Someone will cry (from laughter or old family grievances,
unclear).
Someone will fight for the last piece of pork skin.
Even the Gringos know this.
And some of them might even find it sexy...
only Lord knows why!

If Memory Serves

Step 4: The soundtrack?
Decks of cards slapping on the table.
Sambinha playing too loud from someone's cracked speaker.
Your cousin's boyfriend shouting that they're going vegan…
…right after their third helping.

Step 5: Aftermath.
Tea? Of course not.
Sugary coffee.
Regret? Perhaps.
That slow, sweet bellyache of having eaten too much and feeling
exactly as full
as your heart.

My nature?
It's Brazil.
It's Brasília.
It's hunger and humour.
Salt, sweet, and stubbornness.
A little *saudade*,
a lot of garlic,
and always, always
room for more.

99

John C. Mannone

FLAN MANNONE

*Quilt art hangs on the walls of the high school
where I teach — a patchwork of countries, their
flags stitched together in one colorful apron.*

I walk down the halls
of my high school, see
pride in September postings
on the walls — students
honoring Hispanic culture
of Spanish-speaking nations
around the world. I read
about some famous athletes,
performers, and though
conspicuously missing:
Nobel Prize-winning poets
Pablo Neruda, Octavio Paz,
as well as Latinos/Latinas
from the "hills of science,"
I sing the language of my birth
   quiero volar
   como un pájarito —
and like a little bird, I want
to fly to a eucalyptus tree
in Montevideo, Uruguay
where I was born, and perch
on a branch to smell the salt
from the harbor and listen
to the echoes
of my childhood laughter.

But those trees are only in my
old-man dreams churning
with the green Atlantic
by steam-driven propellers
of *SS Brasil* emigrating me
to *Los Estados Unidos.*

If Memory Serves

I return to South America,
to Argentina for the rest of my
toddler years before coming back
with my dear sister, Lidia.

       Now, I am Latino
my identity resurrected
despite my "perfect" English
and my Spanish in disrepair,
but those words will never leave
my tongue, even though I tried
to chase them away when I was five:
           ¡No hablas a mi en español
           cuando soy con mis amigos!
I'd complain to my Sicilian-born
parents to only to speak to me in *inglés*
around my newfound Baltimore friends.

But never was I ashamed in bringing
empanadas to school: sugar-sprinkled
crescent pies filled with cumin- and
oregano-seasoned meat with raisins,
olives, and hardboiled eggs, or
           milanesas de pollo —
    I can still taste the grated Romano
    cheese mixed with breadcrumbs,
    the egg-washed chicken flaked with parsley,
         then for dessert, a slathering
         of *membrillo* — quince jam —
         on a slice of Moranto's Italian bread.
All as delicious as any poem in my mouth.

           ~~~

In the teacher's lounge, I eat
           un pedaso de matambre
           arrollado
thin flank steak stuffed and rolled,
           ~~~

followed with *yerba mate*. I relax
with that hot tea sipped through
a sculpted metal straw, *una bombilla*,
and savor a dish of flan
the way my mother mastered
making it — dense and delicate custard
in a pool of caramelized sugar.

BREAD BABY

When my son was six days old, I made a loaf of bread, and it healed a piece of me. This is the story of that loaf.

The pregnancy had been hard, contestant nausea coupled with ever-present fear. I carried the loss of my first pregnancy all the way through my second, always on guard, always checking. I could barely eat. Food was a chore, a battle to fight and often lose (which would mean more guilt to impose on myself). I struggled with resenting this little baby, this baby that I wanted so badly, this baby that was making me so miserable.

The birth wasn't any easier, but mercifully, it was safe. I was so exhausted after laboring for days that I barely remember any of it, but I do remember the moment he was placed on my chest. Wet and warm, our hearts still beating as one. I was *so proud* of us in that moment, this little baby and I. We had fought and labored, and we had won. We did something neither of us had ever done before, and we did it together.

The second thing I remember is *hunger*. The cure had been instant, as soon as I pushed him from my body, my appetite returned. I remember laughing, delighted by the forgotten sensation of an appetite, of wanting. *I'm hungry!* I exclaimed. Someone ran to get me food and I swear, Chick-Fil-A never tasted so good.

The first week was hard *(to be honest, the first month was hard, the first year was hard)*. He didn't sleep, my body felt like it had been through a war, and I didn't know what I was doing. It was on one of those bleary-eyed first days that I decided to make bread. Not just any bread, but züpfe. It's not quick, it's not simple, but it is delicious. And more than that, it's a love story.

Züpfe is a traditional Swiss bread, and the women in my family have been making it for generations. I learned to make it from my mother, who learned from her mother, and her mother before her, and so on. It's an enriched dough, made with eggs, milk, and butter. The dough is always braided with a four-strand braid. I remember watching my mom braid it so quickly, hands flying as she tucked and swooped the dough strands. She'd slow it down for me and guide my hands over and over until the rhythm was ingrained in me.

As I made the bread on that cold January day, my new little baby watched from his bassinet (miraculously not crying for a few minutes). I mixed the flour and yeast and all the ingredients and the magical dough came together, as it always does for me. It's such a beautiful dough. Plush and supple and with just the right amount of stretch. I watched it rise as I nursed.

104

When it came time to braid it, my hands were sure and unfaltering. It had been months since I last made züpfe, but it came back to me easily, like my mom and grandma were right there with me, guiding my hands. As I braided, I thought about the endless chain of birthing women. How we are all connected to our mothers. As daughters in the womb, we already carry all our eggs, and so in that form, we were also a part of our grandmother's bodies. An endless braid stretching into the past and future.

The very act of making züpfe gave me strength. It helped me feel normal, like myself, and it helped me remember: motherhood was once new for all the women before me, too. I carry their wisdom in me, and I will pass it on my children. Sometimes with words, sometimes with actions, and sometimes just with bread.

Züpfe Recipe

2 1/4 tsp yeast
2 T. + 2 tsp. warm water
2 c. scalded milk
1/2 c. melted butter
1 1/2 tsp. salt
1/4 c. sugar
2 eggs + 1 egg for wash
7 c. flour

Bloom the yeast in water. In a bowl or stand mixer, combine milk, butter, salt, sugar, 2 eggs. Add the yeast mixture, then mix in a few cups of flour. Add the rest of the flour in increments, kneading until the dough ball cleans the bowl.

Place the dough in a greased bowl, rise until doubled. Divide dough into 4 portions, roll each into a long rope. Using 2 ropes, braid into a 4 strand braided loaf for a traditional design.

On baking sheets lined with parchment, rise the loaves until doubled. Brush on egg wash before baking. Bake at 375°F until browned, about 25-35 minutes. Yield: 2 loaves

STRAWBERRY RASH

Dripping flesh-red through and through, Swedish strawberries are, as my own young daughter tells me with each brimming paper box I bring home, "the goodest in the whole world." 19, 20 hours of sunshine will do that to a berry, and June in Sweden, if granted just one week of warm temperatures, will yield more of those sugary jewels that Swedes wait for, than even a house full of round-bellied toddlers can finish.

Strawberry season is a reprieve from living in this strange, cold land and sweet reward after winter's heavy darknesses. Seeing these shiny berries displaces me. Suddenly, I am back in my apartment in Ann Arbor, Michigan, 22 years old, on the phone with my grandmother, asking her what she would do with an entire flat, about 10 or 12 pounds of the perfectly ripe treats.

I had purchased them impulsively, just one day before departing for a summer visit to the East Coast, where I would see her and the rest of my family. There was no way I could eat that many berries in a single day. *What would she bake, how would she preserve them, what was the best way to enjoy these fragile, fleeting fruits?* My grandmother, warning me, don't eat too many, too quickly — you can get a rash, maybe even an allergy, to the thing you most love. I don't know whether that's true, but my mother's mother, seven years silent now from dementia, can't tell me the story behind this story, can't tell me how she came to know that abundance can lead to suffering.

The living grief of loving someone with dementia means you have to be content with the memories you have. You don't get to create new ones. You don't get to ask about old ones. I have heard others say that this grief of losing someone to dementia comes from its slow-moving nature, how you don't notice how bad it is until it's too far gone, and you haven't realized it was your last chance to be with the person they once were. The loved one is still alive but no longer *there*, and that in-between-ness, the twilight living, is what makes the pain so sharp.

For me, the pain instead comes from a sense of immovability and solidity. *Memory-making* becomes *memories made.* My brain fills in the Swedish: *slut* [pronounced: *sloot*]. Simultaneously past and present, the word means both that something has "run out" and also is "the end." Those marathon dinners at her house — can I remember the taste of her Thanksgiving potatoes, her Sunday meatballs, her chocolate frosting? Home from college, sitting at the small round kitchen table drinking weak, milky coffee, eating crumbly bakery cookies, her warm hand clasping the top of mine. Recipes written in black ink on thin-lined paper, emissaries from that kitchen table to wherever my vagabond self happened to receive them: Lexington, La Honda, Tulsa. *Slut.*

One of the last times my grandmother was cogent, I discussed with her our impending decision to move to Sweden. My husband had the job offer there; my own job offer was in North Carolina. Should I go to North Carolina, live apart from him for some time? Or give up my career and join my husband on an international adventure? *Go to Sweden*, she told me. *Be with your husband.* Her impatient and certain admonishment to prioritize my family gave me the permission to choose to anchor myself to a person and place rather than to a profession. She understood the push-and-pull these competing priorities had manifested in my life to that point, but she could not have understood, nor could I, how moving to Sweden started me down a path from which I could not return. She was on her own path, too. I would never again see her in her power.

* * *

November falls dim and drizzly, the month of my grandmother's birth. I am standing in the afternoon twilight in my modern Scandinavian kitchen, sifting bones to make stock for her chicken soup. I think of her voice that day, gravelly with age and decisive with wisdom, as I sort out the broth's solids, leaving the golden liquid behind. *Go to Sweden.* Seven years have passed; shallow roots have begun spreading their tentative tendrils into the rocky soil of this northern land.

I am making the soup for my daughter, 14 months old. I have not yet made it to my memory's standard, could not yet get the flavor just right. I text my aunt, my sister, who write with tips. *Maybe this time.*

By the time the soup is ready, I sit across from my daughter at the head of our table. I use the large white ceramic spoons common in Asian restaurants; they steadily contain the perfect volume, at the perfect depth, for her tiny mouth. I merely hold it, letting her come to the spoon on her own, her face jutting forward to catch the golden liquid. She puts her warm hand over mine firmly, decisively, bringing the spoon to her waiting mouth, murmuring yum yum yummmmm over and over. I signal my husband to take a video. The video itself a solidification of this memory. I send it to my aunt, my sister. Thank you.

* * *

I always found it curious when people would say, about young children, *oh don't worry; they won't remember* in regard to some aspect of their first years. How do we know what they hold in their minds, in their bodies? As soon as she could speak, I asked my daughter what it felt like to be born. *Att ramla ner,* she answered, in Swedish: like falling down. And before that? *Att vänta.* Like waiting.

Who's to say she can't also remember flavors long before she had the words to describe them? Four years old now, she loves pasta with tomato sauce, something I craved — and ate — often during pregnancy. We know that babies experience flavors in utero, that these early experiences can influence their later tastes. And recent research suggests that the flavors a fetus senses prenatally via amniotic fluid can be specifically remembered for

at least a year after birth: for example, the particular taste of kale
or carrot. Perhaps my daughter's love of tomato sauce, too, was
a kind of destined memory, passed down through the maternal
line: the flavors my mother fed me, perhaps what she fed herself
when pregnant with me, what my grandmother fed her, what
my grandmother ate while pregnant with her? A memory made
solid, through embodied time and fleshy kinship.

We also know that female babies are born with all the eggs
their ovaries will ever hold, so the egg that became my daughter
was inside me while I was inside my mother. And so on,
backward in time. Could the taste of those tomatoes, that
pasta, brought from Calabria to New York and then to Sweden,
be carried in those miniscule cells? Could it be passed forward
to the seeds of my daughter's children, should she choose and
be able to bear them? And what new flavors will be added to
this chain of memory and kin?

* * *

Returning home to Sweden in late June after traveling inter-
nationally for work, I immediately notice the light rash on my
daughter's face. *Her strawberry rash*, my husband noted, as if such
a thing were self-evident. *We've been eating a lot of strawberries.*

I had never mentioned that conversation with my grandmother
to my husband, who I would not meet until years later. I am, at
once, split into two: simultaneously in this moment of reunion,
listening to my daughter's voice and in a kitchen in Ann Arbor,
listening to my grandmother's.

What will home taste like for my child? What memories am I
molding, the days I am too tired from work's grind and buy her
fast-food chicken nuggets, the days we stop at a local café for a
warm cinnamon bun and coffee, the days we walk in the forest
snacking on blueberries (her sleeves, hands, mouth all stained
indigo, violet)?

Will her memories be another way to mark her as "other," the child of two foreign parents? Or will her childhood instead be scented with licorice and chanterelles and saffron, cleaving her from us but cementing her Swedishness and thus, her belonging? She will likely blend the two, just as two languages merge in her mind, remembering peanut butter sandwiches, rhubarb *saft*, Goldfish crackers, cardamom buns, pumpkin pie.

I will remember her first tastes of chicken soup, and I will tell her the story, and I will show her the video, and she will construct a memory of that moment if she does not already have one, and the construction will be indistinguishable from the "real" memory, because, of course, the real memory is also a construction. And every day, new chances, tastes, delights; every day, gratitude. The memories are not solidified, not over. *Vänta*. Wait. June always returns.

RIPENING

What of the hillside olives in October
eager to be shaken loose,
the winter oranges in Kissimmee
clamoring to release into a soft hand?
Rubies swing on trapezes
from every cherry tree in Traverse City
until spring says, *Go!*
Melons yearn for someone
to press their fontanelle.
Sugar Lady peaches dream
of swanning around the farmer's market
like we do, every Saturday — purple plums,
drunk on sunshine, begging to be plucked.

111

What of reckless wanting?
It does no good to rush the ripening.
Let the devastation of cutting
into an avocado that won't yield
warn you of desperate desire.
But waiting — oh, pure ache.
I'd wait to pick you every time.

DON'T PUT NO SUGAR IN MY GRITS

I think it was 1999 because Cash Money was taking over when I had my first unintended sampling of sweet grits. I was in the Navy stationed in Yokosuka, Japan, living my best young life. A dear friend of mine came to the barracks to visit and decided to make the entire crew breakfast; it was customary for my friends to gather in my room.

My last roommate had given me all of her cooking contraband — an electric skillet, toaster oven, a few basic utensils — and I promised to do the right thing with it by making sure all my friends could eat. It was against the rules to cook in the barracks, but tell that to all the chefs who lived there. We had hot plates, a full-sized refrigerator, and all the seasonings you buy next door at the Navy Exchange. The key to ensuring we never got reported was to make a plate for the person on duty that day.

My friends would show up with whatever foods they were craving at the time. And we'd have an old-school get together right there. On any given day, we would have the typical soul food fare, but other times I liked to mix it up. We would have fried rice, chicken Alfredo, even a curry dish. Plenty of years and failed recipes later, I am finally the chef I thought I was back then. Some of those meals just did not make the mark. That's ok, we all got to learn.

Everyone took turns preparing something. This particular day, my home girl from Jersey, Kia, was on duty. This woman was so tiny I could see clearly over her head. She was pregnant and sweeter and bossier than anyone I ever met. That thick East Coast Spanish mingled with AAVE (African-American vernacular or "Ebonics" if you will) — commanded every person around to pay attention.

I played DJ, while she prepared breakfast. Since we'd opted out of church, it was a soulful Sunday brunch full of all the fixings: bacon, sausage, eggs, and grits. I shimmied and praised the Lord a little while listening to her sing (she had a beautiful voice) and bang pots.

After what felt like an eternity, she passed the plates. I went for the grits first, steaming hot and beautifully buttered. I grew up eating grits, but they were not an every-week type of fare. My family preferred the sweetness of oatmeal and Cream of Wheat; we even ate Malt-O-Meal more than grits. But, every time I had the chance to eat grits, I did. Grits have always been THAT breakfast for me. They feel special: Like, "You got griiiiiits!" (insert Jill Scott voice).

I was hungry and ready because this chef loves a meal that I don't have to prepare myself. Kia had never disappointed me before.

I grabbed a forkful of hot steamy grits with a little piece of scrambled egg. What happened next was not my finest moment. Never one to yuck someone's yum, I wanted in my heart of hearts to react better than I did.

But the moment my tongue registered sugar in the grits, my body revolted against me.

If you have ever watched the professional diva-actress Jenifer Lewis — sometimes called the unofficial "Mother of Black Hollywood" and a memorable character in real life — on film, you know the "don't play with me" look I gave my dear friend. I did not have an Afro or a cigarette, but my spirit did.

Please don't judge me; it was a long time ago and I was young. But I spit it out. I spit out the grits. I could not even. At that time, I had no idea that people put sugar in grits. Say that last sentence while clapping in between each word. I was ready to add hot sauce and stir the eggs and sausage right up in there. Instead, I was met with a very confusing blend of sweetness that just did not suit my palate.

I was taken aback. Flabbergasted. Bewildered. Amazed — and not in a good way.

While attempting to gather myself, I realized that I hurt my friend's feelings as she clutched invisible pearls and exhaled audibly and that was not my intention. I never want to upset someone because we have different taste in food. But I just knew that this monstrosity could not be real. I mean, they looked smooth, hot and delicious.

I called home a few days later, and I told my entire family about the grits. We had a good laugh, but that may have been the start of my understanding of regional differences in soul food. Sweet grits were the catalyst to conversations that brought on lively debates of whether fish and spaghetti go together (they do), who washes their meat and why, and what is the deal with mumbo sauce? The best arguments took place between all the Caribbean folk fighting over who makes the best rice. I don't want to start any fights, but I am partial to arroz con gandules myself.

What I learned that day is that, even in the African diaspora, the food culture is wide, and there is room for us all. Everyone else ate the grits and enjoyed them.

I have since attempted to eat sweet grits, to make up to Kia, to atone for my reaction so many years ago. Each time, my reaction is the same. We are still in touch with each other, and I am not sure she remembers that day.

It is safe to say that I will forever declare as I sit at the table: Don't put no sugar in my grits, please. I would rather they be unsalted and bland than sweet. I can fix bland. I cannot fix sweet. But, you, you should eat your grits the way you like them. Pay the haters no mind.

GRILLED PIZZA, 1999

The whole neighborhood fired up gas grills.
We didn't live on a charcoal kind of street.
The woods out back, their many streams,
small ponds, the big river just east,
bloomed mosquitoes like spores in wind;
we scratched our necks and it was summer.

Ma bought supermarket dough,
cut up a bunch of toppings, threw on
one of three CDs we played on months-long repeat.
In New England, you forget how to do June
until it's August, but you remember how heat
never stays, how you'll always need a coat nearby.

The pizza was too good: charred al dente
by the propane-stinking flames. We got it
once a year, once a summer at the soot-stained
porch table while dusk blinked around us.
The crickets and katydids screamed for night,
and the quiet lights of the sky exploded.

115

POSTMORTEM

The man who killed my sister interrupted her lunch at Chili's, sliding into her booth. She was working on her laptop, per usual. *Always working.* He introduced himself and flirted over Southwestern egg rolls and Technicolor margaritas. Her beauty arrested him, he said with a vulturine smile. She was charmed.

Later, at their debut as a couple before our family, the man who killed my sister curled his lip in disgust. Who put sunflower seeds on a salad? He shoved the offending dish to the edge of the table. There was nothing edible on this Southern brasserie's menu, he declared. And the waiter had "sugar in his blood." He sneer-laughed at his own joke, letting his hand dangle limply from his arm in the old, unmistakable slur. I said, "Our family doesn't talk like that." My usually opinionated sister looked down at the table.

The man who killed my sister didn't know how to pronounce "sriracha" when he ordered the spicy burger at Denny's, one of the few places our large family could eat in this rural town. I couldn't resist darting a look at our other sister. He saw the glance and knew he would never be one of us, bourgeois over-educated people that we are, comfortable with foreign words on menus and the art of ordering. My sister paid for our snobbery.

The man who killed my sister married her. She was 50 and wanted the "Mrs. Degree" more than any of her professional achievements: the multiple master's degrees, the high-powered job managing millions at a regional nonprofit, national accolades for her work. In an unplanned lunch intervention with our mother, she screamed, "But I love him!" and stormed away. The cafe manager glided smoothly to our table and inquired, in hushed hospitality-speak, if everything was alright. We pretended he was asking about the sandwiches.

The man who killed my sister declared he was allergic to peanuts — unless they were covered by caramel (a Snickers was therefore nonlethal and permissible for consumption). He could only eat green apples. Should a red one graze his lips, he would perish. I suddenly longed for a Red Delicious. When he discovered chestnuts in the Thanksgiving stuffing, he declared a sudden universal nut allergy and ran to the bathroom. Loud, vaudevillian retching ensued offstage. An Agatha Christie villain would have solved the problem of him with a surreptitious dose of real almond extract in the flourless chocolate cake or a undetectable dusting of peanuts in the banana pudding. We joked about murder by allergy in phone conversations and that the NSA was listening. No menu could ever mollify him. Fictional food sensitivities made him the main character and victim of every meal.

117

The man who killed my sister managed a fast food restaurant, when he worked. My sister arrived at closing to sweep the floors after her own full day of work. He needed a helpmate who could take body blows and still glad-hand like the first lady hosting the holiday party. My sister could not cook and clean enough for him, her preordained role. After all, he was a man and a jackleg preacher. She was just Adam's cast-off rib.

The man who killed my sister shut himself in that same restaurant and threatened to kill himself when she balked at all the times he knocked her head into their townhome's walls. The neighbors on the other side of the wall got used to the noise. My sister got used to the concussions. She grew confused and toddly on her feet.

The man who killed my sister wanted to open his own restaurant with her money. He bellowed that she never supported him. She was a Madonna when he got what he wanted - her body, her submission, her fear. But most often, she was just like his mother, who had been a single parent who brought men home and sold her body to feed her five sons. Like all women ultimately, both were unredeemable whores.

Dressed for work, my sister died under her kitchen table from a "brain event." Her death certificate suggests nothing malevolent or untoward, no immediately precipitating violence or head trauma. But her brain and skull were a warren of old injuries. My sister had finally escaped the man who slowly killed her with stress and beatings. They'd been divorced less than a month, and in the last week of her life, she called all her friends and bubbled with life and light. Five bathing suits hung in her closet, price tags still on, for the vacations she'd planned. Her pantry was stocked. He'd call her and say he had no money for food. Sometimes, she sent him cash. She didn't want him to starve to death.

THANK YOU TO THE FOLLOWING PUBLICATIONS AND VENUES WHERE VERSIONS OF THESE PIECES FIRST APPEARED:

"The Winter Feast" by Aharon Levy first appeared in *Duende*

"Watermelon Seeds" by Eric Paul Shaffer first appeared in *Oregon Literary Review, Volume 2, Number 1 (Winter/Spring, 2007)*, and in the author's book *A Million-Dollar Bill (2018)*

"Buon Appetito" by Christy Hartman first appeared in *Frazzled Lit, Issue 1*

"Wonderland" by Ellen Estilai first appeared in *2020 Writing from Inlandia,* published by Inlandia Institute

"Challah" by Jan Berlfein Burns was first read at *The Braid*, spoken word theatre in Santa Monica, CA

"Your Hands Look Different Now" by Chris Nigro first appeared in *Serving Up: Essays on Food, Identity and Culture*, published by Unbound, an imprint of Boundless Publishing Group

DR. CYNTHIA GREENLEE is an award-winning journalist and historian whose work explores the intersections of food, history, and culture. A James Beard Award winner, she has written for *The Atlantic*, *The New York Times*, *Smithsonian*, and more. Her work has appeared in multiple Best American Food Writing anthologies. Formerly deputy editor at the Southern Foodways Alliance and senior editor at The Counter, she is currently working on a book rethinking Black foodways in the South. A lifelong Southerner by birth, rearing and choice, she draws inspiration from her heritage and deep roots in North and South Carolina.

GOOD PRINTED THINGS is a small press based in Greenville, South Carolina. Since 2018, Good Printed Things has published works focused on connection – with ourselves, others, and the surrounding world. Specializing in small print runs, we proudly work with emergent and established writers and artists to seek out, explore, and celebrate the good.

Other Good Printed Things anthologies include:

Not The Way You Expect: A Collection of Words on Motherhood
Holding Patterns: A Collection of Words on Ritual